ALL FOR ME

(A Hayden Smart Mystery—Book 1)

Rylie Dark

Rylie Dark

Bestselling author Rylie Dark is author of the SADIE PRICE FBI SUSPENSE THRILLER series, comprising six books; of the CARLY SEE FBI SUSPENSE THRILLER series, comprising six books; of the MIA NORTH FBI SUSPENSE THRILLER series, comprising six books; of the MORGAN STARK FBI SUSPENSE THRILLER series, comprising five books; of the HAILEY ROCK FBI SUSPENSE THRILLER series, comprising eight books; of the TARA STRONG MYSTERY series, comprising six books; of the ALEX QUINN FBI SUSPENSE THRILLER series, comprising five books; of the MAEVE SHARP FBI SUSPENSE THRILLER, comprising five books; of the KELLY CRUZ FBI SUSPENSE THRILLER, comprising five books; of the JESSIE REACH FBI SUSPENSE THRILLER, comprising seven books (and counting); of the BECCA THORN FBI SUSPENSE THRILLER, comprising five books (and counting); of the CASEY FAITH SUSPENSE THRILLER, comprising five books (and counting); of the ARIA BRANDT SUSPENSE THRILLER, comprising five books (and counting); and of the new HAYDEN SMART SUSPENSE THRILLER, comprising five books (and counting).

An avid reader and lifelong fan of the mystery and thriller genres, Rylie loves to hear from you, so please feel free to visit www.ryliedark.com to learn more and stay in touch.

ISBN: 978-1-0943-8609-6

BOOKS BY RYLIE DARK

HAYDEN SMART MYSTERY
ALL FOR ME (Book #1)
ALL FOR NOTHING (Book #2)
ALL FOR VENGEANCE (Book #3)
ALL FOR YOU (Book #4)
ALL FOREVER (Book #5)

ARIA BRANDT MYSTERY
THE UNKNOWN WOMAN (Book #1)
THE UNKNOWN WIFE (Book #2)
THE UNKNOWN NEIGHBOR (Book #3)
THE UNKNOWN GUEST (Book #4)
THE UNKNOWN PAST (Book #5)

CASEY FAITH MYSTERY
BEHIND HIS EYES (Book #1)
BEHIND HIS SMILE (Book #2)
BEHIND HIS MASK (Book #3)
BEHIND HIS LIES (Book #4)
BEHIND HIS THOUGHTS (Book #5)

BECCA THORN MYSTERY
GONE COLD (Book #1)
GONE DARK (Book #2)
GONE SILENT (Book #3)
GONE HOLLOW (Book #4)
GONE FOREVER (Book #5)

JESSIE REACH MYSTERY
HIS OTHER SIDE (Book #1)
HIS OTHER SELF (Book #2)
HIS OTHER SECRET (Book #3)
HIS OTHER WISH (Book #4)
HIS OTHER PLAN (Book #5)

KELLY CRUZ MYSTERY
WHERE YOU GO (Book #1)
WHERE YOU HIDE (Book #2)
WHERE YOU SLEEP (Book #3)
WHERE YOU RUN (Book #4)
WHERE YOU FEAR (Book #5)

MAEVE SHARP FBI SUSPENSE THRILLER
WITH MALICE (Book #1)
WITH ENVY (Book #2)
WITH VENGEANCE (Book #3)
WITH RAGE (Book #4)
WITH YOU (Book #5)

ALEX QUINN SUSPENSE THRILLER
FIRST, MURDER (Book #1)
SECOND, DEATH (Book #2)
THIRD, ENVY (Book #3)
FOURTH, LUST (Book #4)
FIFTH, WRATH (Book #5)

TARA STRONG MYSTERY
GIRL WITHOUT A CHANCE (Book #1)
GIRL WITHOUT A HOME (Book #2)
GIRL WITHOUT A TRACE (Book #3)
GIRL WITHOUT A NAME (Book #4)
GIRL WITHOUT A PRAYER (Book #5)
GIRL WITHOUT A PAST (Book #6)

HAILEY ROCK FBI SUSPENSE THRILLER
BEHIND YOU (Book #1)
BESIDE YOU (Book #2)
AFTER YOU (Book #3)
WATCHING YOU (Book #4)
JUDGING YOU (Book #5)
FOLLOWING YOU (Book #6)

SADIE PRICE FBI SUSPENSE THRILLER
ONLY MURDER (Book #1)
ONLY RAGE (Book #2)
ONLY HIS (Book #3)

ONLY ONCE (Book #4)
ONLY SPITE (Book #5)
ONLY MADNESS (Book #6)

MIA NORTH FBI SUSPENSE THRILLER
SEE HER RUN (Book #1)
SEE HER HIDE (Book #2)
SEE HER SCREAM (Book #3)
SEE HER VANISH (Book #4)
SEE HER GONE (Book #5)
SEE HER DEAD (Book #6)

CARLY SEE FBI SUSPENSE THRILLER
NO WAY OUT (Book #1)
NO WAY BACK (Book #2)
NO WAY HOME (Book #3)
NO WAY LEFT (Book #4)
NO WAY UP (Book #5)
NO WAY TO DIE (Book #6)

MORGAN STARK FBI SUSPENSE THRILLER
TOO LATE (Book #1)
TOO CLOSE (Book #2)
TOO FAR GONE (Book #3)
TOO LOST (Book #4)
TOO BROKEN (Book #5)

PROLOGUE

Laura Henley's breath came out in a long, controlled exhale, her palms pressing together at heart center, a silent namaste to the sultry room. Even though she made her living helping people relax and release the tension of the previous day, she often found that she needed a moment to herself at the end of each yoga class she taught. She imagined that it was just her in the studio, as she focused on her breath and the steadiness of the mat underneath her.

The heat of the studio seemed to permeate every cell of her body, turning her muscles to molten rubber and her skin to a sheen of sweat that threatened her grip on the slick surface of her mat. She could feel a drop sliding down her spine as she held the final pose, the serenity of her vinyasa flow juxtaposed against the oppressive warmth enveloping her.

She allowed herself to be more present with the class. Many of the people in the back were improving with every week, and her guidance had helped them live a more holistic life.

"Let's transition into savasana." Her voice was a gentle hum in the heated space, steady despite the droplets beading at her forehead.

She watched as her students followed suit, their bodies unfurling gracefully onto their backs, eyes closed, arms by their sides. The sea of chests rising and falling was hypnotic, a testament to the shared energy they had created here in this sacred space.

Even though she found peace here, her life up until this point had been anything but tranquil. A series of failed relationships, jobs, and friendships had led her to look to yoga and meditation to find inner peace. She became an instructor almost by accident.

Moving with deliberate tranquility, Laura reached for the mallet beside the Tibetan singing bowl perched on a small stool near the front of the class. With a practiced motion, she struck the gong, its deep, resonant soundwaves billowing through the air like a sonic embrace. The vibrations seemed to ripple across the room, cradling her students in an audible cocoon of peace.

As the tones faded into a hush, Laura spoke, her words floating over her class like a benediction.

“Thank you for being present with me today. And more importantly, for showing up for yourselves.”

A deep exhale sounded in the room.

“Return your mind to the intention you set at the beginning of class today. Remember to trust your body. Your intuition.”

Another deep breath. She knew that even though the others were there, she was really speaking to herself.

“I want to end our time together with a few affirmations. You can repeat if it feels right, or simply let the words wash over you.”

This was her favorite part of every class.

"I am strong," she affirmed, believing in the power these simple phrases held to bolster and heal. "I am safe," she continued, the soft cadence of her voice wrapping around each student, a verbal caress meant to soothe and protect. "I am loved," she concluded, a reminder of their intrinsic worth, a call to self-compassion that would linger in their minds long after they rolled up their mats and stepped back out into the world.

In the dim light, with the scent of incense still clinging to the humid air, Laura stood as a beacon of calm, embodying the very affirmations she bestowed upon her class.

The gentle hum of the air conditioning unit broke the stillness as it whirred back to life, a welcome reprieve from the sweltering heat that had accumulated within the studio. Laura watched with satisfaction as her students stirred from their meditative repose, slowly rolling onto their sides and pushing themselves up into a seated position. The overhead lights flickered on, casting a warm glow that seemed to chase away the last tendrils of shadow from the corners of the room.

"Take a moment to ground yourselves before you go," she instructed, her voice a soft echo in the now-cooling space. "Remember, your practice doesn't end here; it's a part of you, wherever you are."

With smiles of gratitude, they began to collect their belongings, the sounds of zippers and Velcro filling the air alongside the muted thumps of mats being rolled up. Laura moved among them, her bare feet silent on the studio floor, offering individual farewells to each of her regulars. As she approached Mark, whose dedication had grown leaps and bounds since he first stepped into her class, she couldn't help but share an encouraging nod.

"Mark, your focus was exceptional today," she told him, her eyes sparkling with pride. "You're nearly there with the handstand. Just a little more practice, and you'll nail it."

His face lit up, his earlier frustration at his wobbling attempts transformed into renewed determination. "Thanks, Laura. I'll get it next time," he replied, buoyed by her confidence in him.

One by one, they filtered out, leaving behind only the memories of their shared energy, until Laura was alone with the silence once more. She took a deep breath, letting the tranquility wash over her as she began to tidy the space. Wiping down the blocks and disinfecting the straps, she worked methodically, restoring order to the studio that served as both her sanctuary and her livelihood.

Finally, only her mat lay sprawled across the floor—a vibrant splash of turquoise against the polished wood. Her mat had become like an old friend over the last few months. She bent to roll it, her movements fluid and practiced, securing it with the attached elastic bands

She waited until all her students left before completing the final tasks of her shift. As the last one there, she put all the towels in the washing machine, sprayed the studio with a floral room spray, and wiped down the windows. Outside, all the other businesses in their small strip mall were closed, and the parking lot was almost empty.

With one final glance around the room, ensuring nothing was amiss, Laura picked up her mat and walked towards the door.

Her hand paused on the lock, fingers brushing over the cool metal as she cast a look over her shoulder, the echo of affirmations whispering through her mind. Turning the key, she heard the decisive click that signaled the end of another day's journey. The door closed with a gentle thud behind her, the sound sealing the studio in its own cocoon of potential until the next sunrise beckoned new growth and new beginnings.

Laura stepped out into the night, her yoga mat tucked under her arm. The comforting hum of the air conditioning from the studio faded behind her as the door clicked shut, replaced by a stillness that seemed to blanket the world outside. She squinted into the darkness; the streetlight that usually illuminated the parking lot was out, leaving the asphalt ocean an inky black, disturbed only by the distant glow of the strip mall signage.

A shiver ran up her spine, a whisper of unease that prickled at the edges of her consciousness.

She told all her students to listen to their intuitions, but she didn't want to listen to her own at that moment. A terrible feeling crept up her spine.

Laura's gaze darted across the expanse of parked cars to where she had left hers in the morning—a solitary shape on the far side of the lot. The shadows seemed deeper tonight, more pronounced, as if they were waiting to swallow her whole.

Even if her every nerve had screamed to go back to the studio, there was nothing she could do about it. She had to get home.

"I am strong," she murmured to herself, the mantra slipping quietly between her lips. Her voice felt small, almost lost in the vast silence. Clasping her hands, she took a deep, steadying breath—the kind she taught to her students—allowing her diaphragm to expand fully before exhaling slowly. She wanted to believe in the power of her own affirmations, to let them build a fortress around her heart.

But with each step she took, her heart thudded louder against her ribcage, a drumbeat of trepidation that refused to go away. "I am strong," she repeated internally, trying to match the rhythm of her steps to the cadence of her breathing. It was a technique meant to center and empower, yet tonight it felt like a thin veil against the creeping dread that threatened to unravel her calm.

Laura quickened her pace, the sound of her own shoes against the pavement a staccato punctuation in the quiet. All around her, the empty space of the parking lot seemed to press in, tangible and oppressive, as if charged with the anticipation of something unseen. Her fingers tightened around the strap of her mat, the texture suddenly grounding. She was so close now, just a few more strides to safety, to the familiar confines of her car, to the promise of light and motion and the dispelling of shadows.

Laura's fingers curled around the keys in her palm, their cool metal edges pressing into her skin.

If worst came to worst, she could try her best to defend herself.

She wondered if perhaps she was just hyper-sensitive to some bad energy in the area and that nothing really wanted to harm her.

A silent mantra began to form in her mind as she visualized the comforting end to her evening: soon she would be home, the soft glow of her kitchen lights welcoming her back to safety.

She imagined the sizzle of vegetables in a pan, the aroma of garlic and herbs wafting through her small apartment. Her dog, Max, with his warm, trusting eyes, would be waiting to greet her at the door, his tail wagging in that steady rhythm that always managed to thaw the chill from her bones.

In her mind's eye, she saw herself sinking into the worn cushions of her couch, Max's head resting on her lap, his presence an anchor in the quiet night. The TV would murmur in the background as she picked at her late dinner, the familiar scenes of a well-loved show playing out before her. Then, just before sleep claimed her, she'd feel Max's weight against her side, his soft breathing syncing with her own, lulling her into a sense of peace, a fortress against the world outside.

With each step towards her car, Laura's grip on the keys tightened, the sharp jangle a whispered promise of imminent departure. Just a few more paces, and she would unlock the door, slide inside, and leave the darkened lot behind.

But the solitude of the parking lot was suddenly shattered by a presence.

Without warning, Laura felt a rush of air, a shift in the atmosphere. Her instincts screamed for her to turn, to confront whatever dared invade her bubble of imagined safety.

Heart pounding, she spun on her heel, and the scene she had painted in her mind evaporated.

Instead, she found herself staring up into the impassive face of a tall man.

He was cloaked in shadows, his attire a void that swallowed the scant light around them. His features were obscured, but there was no mistaking the intent in his stance, the purposeful way he filled the space between them.

Before a scream could claw its way up her throat, his hand was there, cold and suffocating, clamped over her mouth with a pressure that spoke of strength and determination. Laura's eyes widened in terror, her body frozen as primal fear surged through her veins. Her keys, once a symbol of escape, now lay forgotten, just out of reach, as darkness closed in around her.

CHAPTER ONE

Hayden Smart's fingers brushed against the cold surface of her apartment wall, tracing the pictures of faces she knew better than her own.

The space was stark, save for the sketches that hung there — a gallery of ghosts from cases past, each one meticulously detailed and annotated with dates and notes in her tight, angular handwriting.

She had been living in this Seattle apartment for two years, but for the most part it was sparsely decorated. Though she had an old thrift store couch in one corner and some dishes in the kitchen she'd had since college, the space was mostly decorated with her own drawings from crime scenes and old cases. They served as a testament to her relentless pursuit of justice, each drawing a chapter in her ongoing story, a story punctuated by frustration and resolve.

The evening light waned, casting long shadows across the room, playing over the contours of drawn faces that seemed to shift and mutter in the dimming illumination. Among them was the visage of a man with eyes like voids and a smile that never reached them. She didn't know his name, only the havoc he'd wreaked; his face was etched into her memory as indelibly as it was on the paper before her.

As Hayden stood looking at these illustrations of human malevolence, the unidentifiable man's sketch seemed to demand her attention more than the others.

It was not just a reminder of the evil that lurked in the city's underbelly; it was a personal affront, a challenge to her intellect and her badge. Her gaze lingered on the unknown features as if willing them to reveal their secrets, to whisper the name that had eluded her for so long.

She had only gotten a short look at him when he took her sister away years ago, but it had been enough. Ever since, she had been obsessively drawing him, hoping that it would one day help bring him to justice.

Her sister hadn't been seen or heard from in over a decade.

And Hayden didn't like to think about what that meant.

But even if she couldn't find her sister, maybe she could locate the man who took her.

She leaned back against one of the walls. Her vision was starting to blur.

The apartment's sparse furnishing in addition to the couch that had never molded to her form included a small table bearing no rings from casual cups of coffee and a lamp that offered light but no warmth. It mirrored the austerity of her mission. No trinkets or souvenirs cluttered the space. Only purpose lived here, and that purpose was etched in graphite and shadow on the walls that enclosed her. Yet even with the constant images of killers all around her, this place still felt like home.

The city's nocturnal pulse throbbed faintly against Hayden's windows as she declined yet another call with a gentle tap on her phone's screen. "Not tonight," she murmured, more to the room than to herself. The glow of streetlamps seeped through the blinds, casting bars of amber light that striped the bare floor of her apartment. She drew the curtains closed with a swift motion, shutting out the beckoning chaos of Seattle nightlife.

With a sigh, Hayden settled onto the worn fabric of her couch, legs curling beneath her. Her fingers found the plush fur of her cat, a sleek creature named Pissarro, who had claimed the adjacent cushion as his throne. As she stroked him, the rhythmic purring resonated softly in the quiet space, offering a semblance of companionship that humans seldom matched.

Her eyes lifted from the contented feline to the wall where danger and despair were immortalized in shades of gray. Among the faces that stared back, one in particular seized her attention again. This sketch always seemed to be watching her movements. It portrayed a man whose features were ordinary, forgettable even, if not for the coldness in his eyes, the sinister twist of his mouth. That face, which had become a fixture in her life, belonged to the ghost from her past, the man who had torn her sister from their world when Hayden was just sixteen.

In the silence of her solitude, the weight of years spent chasing shadows pressed down on her. She tried to shake off the chill that crept up her spine as she gazed at the drawing. The specter of him was a constant reminder of the day her life had fractured, a catalyst that had shaped her into the woman she was now—obsessive, relentless, solitary. With each glance, the line between hunter and haunted blurred, leaving her to wonder if she was ever truly alone in the room.

The police and FBI had run her sketch through whatever facial recognition programs they could, but it all came up with nothing.

Pissarro, sensing the shift in her mood, nuzzled against her hand, grounding her in the present. Hayden took a deep breath and allowed the familiarity of her cat's presence to anchor her. In this moment, within these walls, she found strength in knowing that some things remained constant, even when the world outside spun in unpredictable spirals.

Maybe it was time for a break from thinking about all of this. Solving crimes and catching the people who perpetrated them was already her full-time job. It shouldn't be her only hobby as well.

Hayden reached for the remote, her fingers brushing over the cool plastic before she grasped it firmly. The television flickered to life with a low hum, casting a bluish glow across the sparsely decorated living room. She sank into the fraying cushions of her worn sofa, the fabric whispering beneath her as she settled in.

On screen, the city's skyline illuminated the night, a testament to the sleepless pulse of Seattle. A seasoned anchor appeared, his expression somber as he began reciting the day's headlines. Hayden leaned forward, her elbows on her knees, eyes intent and searching for anything that might lead to a break in her sister's long-cold case.

"Another day, another litany of crimes," she murmured, more to herself than to Pissarro, who had curled up at the other end of the couch. Despite the comfort of her cat's presence, tension knotted her shoulders as she listened. She dissected each story, hunting for patterns, links, any clue that could guide her toward the man who had become her nemesis.

Years of police sketches and FBI training had honed her eye for detail, yet the face that haunted her — the face that stared down from her wall — remained nameless, elusive. Each crime report was a potential key, each incident a possibility that her search might finally end.

But tonight, like so many nights before, the news cycled through without a whisper of him. With every passing second, her hope flickered and dimmed, like the city lights against the encroaching dawn. She felt the grip of the decade-long obsession tightening. It was the same relentless drive that had propelled her from a grief-stricken teenager into a determined agent, yet even that resolve had its limits.

"Come on, give me something," she whispered, a plea to an indifferent screen. But as the clock ticked on, only the familiar stories of thefts and frauds paraded before her, a carousel of misdeeds that offered no solace, no answers.

Hayden flicked off the TV with a sigh, the drone of the news anchor's voice fading into silence. The glow from countless windows and streetlamps bled through her apartment's sheer curtains, casting a lattice of shadows across the bare walls. Each shadow seemed to echo the faces she had sketched, but tonight, they offered no secrets.

She leaned over to where her sketch pad lay on the coffee table, its cover worn from constant use. As her fingers traced the edges of the paper, a sense of calm began to seep through her. Hayden pulled the pad toward her, flipping it open to a clean page. A pencil, sharp and ready, rolled between her fingers as if it were an extension of her will.

With a deep breath, she let her gaze drift over the urban landscape outside. Buildings rose like jagged teeth against the night sky, their outlines softened by the city's ever-present mist. She translated the view into graphite lines, the skyline unfolding beneath her hand. Each stroke was both a release and a tether, grounding her in the moment while freeing her from the thoughts that constantly prowled the back of her mind.

The pencil danced lightly, capturing the essence rather than the specifics, a contrast of dark shapes and the negative space they defined. Her hand moved with assurance born of years spent sketching suspects and scenes, each line a whisper of something more than just a building or a window. It was Seattle's pulse that she sought to ensnare, the vibrant heartbeat of a city that never truly slept.

The sharp trill of her phone shattered the tranquility. Her hand paused mid-stroke, leaving a trail of graphite dust to settle on the page. Hayden eyed the caller ID; it was Marcus Doyle, her partner at the bureau whose timing had a habit of being either impeccable or inconvenient.

"Smart," she answered, the word a mix of greeting and resignation.

"Doyle here. We've got a situation," came the terse reply, his voice edged with urgency. "There's been a murder—looks messy. I need you at the scene."

Without hesitation, Hayden closed her sketch pad, the incomplete skyline forgotten. "Text me the address. I'll be there in twenty."

"Thanks, Hayden. Be careful," he added before ending the call.

She stood up swiftly, a practiced motion that had her coat on and her badge clipped to her belt in seconds. The cat, disturbed by her sudden movement, gave a plaintive meow as if sensing the shift in energy.

"Keep the fort warm for me," Hayden murmured, giving the feline a brief scratch behind the ears. Then, she strode out the door, her mind already shifting gears from artist to agent, ready to face whatever awaited her in the city's darkened streets.

CHAPTER TWO

The neon sign of the Midnight Brew flickered, casting a sporadic glow on the tired faces in line. Hayden shuffled forward, her gaze landing on a familiar figure just ahead, shoulders squared as if bracing against the night's chill.

She waited a few moments before she saw her partner move inside.

"Marcus," she called out softly, not wanting to startle him amid the low murmur of nocturnal patrons.

He turned, a weary smile spreading across his face. "Hayden!" He stepped forward to give her a short hug.

She had suggested they meet here, a favorite spot for coffee, before investigating the crime scene.

She fell into step beside him as the line inched towards the counter, the scent of strong coffee wrapping around them like a shared secret.

The two liked to meet here before heading to a crime scene. It allowed them a moment to talk and collect their thoughts before diving into to a new case. Not to mention, Hayden relied on the coffee, and nowhere was open later.

"They did warn us when we joined about the long hours and thankless overtime," she answered. She stepped up to the counter and ordered her usual. A flat white with just a drizzle of honey. He ordered too, a black coffee with a single sugar packet.

“I still don’t get how you drink it like that,” she said.

“What can I say? I like to suffer.”

"So, what's with the get-up?" she asked, looking up and down at his outfit.

He was wearing dark jeans and a blue button up with a tailored sport coat. He had even put on a nice watch. And Hayden thought she smelled cologne.

“Did you join a late-night country club and forget to tell me?”

Marcus sighed, fidgeting with his phone before slipping it into his coat pocket. “A late-night country club?"

“Or whatever it was that made you break out that watch.”

He smirked. “I do have a life, you know.”

Hayden picked up her coffee from the counter.

“If you must know, I was on a date. And before you ask, it was a disaster.”

"Disaster?" Hayden arched an eyebrow, her interest piqued as they waited for their order. She knew that she was about to spend the next few days thinking only about murder and death. Maybe a lighthearted story would cheer her up.

"Blind dates always are," he muttered, grabbing his coffee. "My brother's bright idea to set me up with a friend of his. Let's just say our definitions of 'fun' didn't quite align."

"Okay, well, now you have to tell me."

“Turns out, she has about ten pet snakes.”

“Ooh,” Hayden winced for him.

“Why does my brother always set me up with the most bizarre people?”

“Because they’re the only ones who can work around an FBI agent’s terrible schedule,” she answered flatly. Even though she spoke with confidence, she didn’t have much to go on when it came to dating.

“You’re probably right,” he said.

"I’m sorry to hear that," Hayden said, suppressing a smirk as she pictured Marcus enduring what must have been a painfully mismatched encounter.

"Thanks. I survived, though," Marcus added with a shrug. "At least I got the call to come in to work and I didn’t have to suffer through dessert, or another story about her many trips to a water park."

She smiled. “Well, she sounds lovely.”

“What were you up to?”

“Uhh…” she stopped short, unsure how to explain her wall of drawings. It was part of her process as a detective, how she had learned to observe and understand the world around her, but she knew that to everyone else her compulsive drawing of suspects probably seemed manic and a little bit obsessive.

“I was drawing,” she said. “And then I was going to turn in. We still have all that paperwork to finish up from that last case.”

“Don’t remind me,” he said. “You know anything about this case yet?”

Hayden shook her head, cradling her own steaming cup. "Deputy director Wells didn’t tell me much. Just that a body has been found in the park. Female. No witnesses."

Irene had been deputy director of the Seattle FBI field office for a few months, and she was already trying to get her investigators to look into the most interesting cases she could find. With a case like this one and its unusual circumstances, the local police were all too happy to hand it over to the FBI.

"I guess we'll have to get to the scene to know more," he said, and they both stepped aside for the next customers, the warmth from the café contrasting sharply with the cool air that greeted them outside.

"After you," Hayden gestured towards the exit, where the city awaited with its secrets cloaked in shadows. "Park isn't far. Want to just walk?"

"Can't hurt."

The night stretched before them, an inky canvas splashed with the neon artistry of open signs and streetlights. They found their rhythm on the pavement, their footsteps a familiar percussion against the city's nocturne.

Marcus cast a sidelong glance at Hayden, "How's life outside the files and forensics?"

Hayden smiled faintly, aware of her reputation as the embodiment of dedication—or, as some would whisper behind raised coffee cups, obsession. Most of the time, when she got back from work, she was too tired to do anything but go straight to sleep. She knew she should invest more in her personal life, but in her line of work, there just weren't enough hours in the day.

"Actually, I've been doing more lately," she lied. Marcus was always telling her to get out more. See the world. Meet people. "I joined a yoga class."

"Yoga?" Marcus's eyebrow arched in surprise. "I didn't think you were the type."

She wasn't.

"Neither did I," she confessed, feeling a slight twinge of vulnerability. "But stretching in ways I didn't know was possible is oddly... soothing."

"Uh-huh." He nodded slowly, his expression unreadable in the ephemeral dance of shadow and light.

"Well, hopefully this next case is open and shut."

Hayden welcomed the change in topic, her mind already flipping through mental files, ready to dissect lab results and witness statements.

They rounded the corner, the city's pulse thrumming beneath their feet, partners in pursuit of truth hidden in the shadows.

The chill of the late evening air nipped at Hayden as she and Marcus moved with purpose through the streets, their footsteps synched in a silent rhythm. She turned onto a street lined on both sides with beautiful trees, though she couldn't see them well in the dark. The city's never-ending hum served as a backdrop to their hushed anticipation, the night pregnant with unresolved mysteries.

She could see police lights flashing in the distance, where the body had been found on one of the park benches.

Hayden's phone vibrated against her side, jarring her from her thoughts. She glanced at the screen—Wells's name flashed with an urgency that tightened her gut. With a flick of her thumb, she answered. "Hayden."

"Congratulations on the promotion, Director Wells," she managed, her voice even, masking the trepidation that settled like sediment in her stomach. Irene Wells was now the deputy director, a fact that could mean either windfall or wildfire for Hayden's cases.

"Save the pleasantries, Hayden," came the crisp response, the new rank in Irene's tone unmistakable. She dove right into the heart of the matter. "Just checking in."

"I just met Marcus. We're almost to the crime scene."

"Good. I wanted to tell you that I spoke to the local PD."

Hayden pursed her lips. She knew that Wells was eager to make sure that things were done right and to prove herself as the new deputy director, but she didn't appreciate the oversight. "We don't know the cause of death. Probably poison, because there are no lacerations or head injuries that we can see yet. But, of course, we'll need the coroner's report to be sure."

Hayden knew that she was perfectly capable of coming to that conclusion for herself. Did Wells not trust her?

"And I've just learned that there aren't any security cameras in the area."

"I know that you're worried about this case," she said, "but Marcus and I have it under control."

Marcus caught her eye, brow raised in silent question, but Hayden kept her gaze fixed ahead, her jaw set.

"Fine," said Wells. "But I want you to make sure that this one is solved quickly."

"Understood," Hayden replied curtly, the words tasting like lead on her tongue.

The line went dead before Hayden had the chance to argue, to question, to brace herself for the inevitable clash of wills with Wells.

"Are you two going to be able to work together?" asked Marcus.

"It will be fine," said Hayden, with a tight smile. She and Irene had butted heads in the past. This was usually due to a combination of Hayden's unstructured thinking and Irene's constant pressure to solve cases quickly, no matter who got caught in the crossfire. Hayden usually preferred to work without any pressure, coming to her conclusions naturally without being forced into them.

She pocketed her phone, her eyes meeting Marcus's, who was now looking at her expectantly. "Poisoning," she said succinctly, the gravity of the case pulling at her resolve. "Rather than external wounds."

"Damn," Marcus muttered under his breath, his earlier nonchalance replaced by a hard edge. "That complicates matters."

"Complicates is an understatement," Hayden replied as they picked up the pace, the weight of the night's task settling over them like a shroud. They were heading into the belly of the beast, where science met silence, and every answer unearthed only created more questions.

Hayden's footsteps echoed on the damp pavement as they neared the park, her brain churning through the scant details of the case.

She made it to the crowd of police officers around the nearby park bench.

One of them walked over to her. He had a mustache and looked like he had been on the clock for the last forty-eight hours.

"You the feds?" he said to both of them.

"That's us."

"Good. Glad you could make it before we move the body."

"Do you have an ID yet?" she asked.

"A yoga instructor—Laura Henley."

Marcus looked over at her. "That's ironic."

Hayden ignored him.

Yoga was about balance and tranquility, not a usual catalyst for murder. Could it be a disgruntled client? An envious competitor? Or maybe something more personal?

"Seems like an unlikely target," she said.

"A few of our guys suggested poison as the cause of death," said the officer.

“We heard,” said Hayden. “I’d like to request an immediate examination of the body.”

“Well, yeah. Of course. But that’s not the weird part.”

Hayden looked over at Marcus, then back to the officer. “What is the weird part?”

“Well, for that, you’ll have to take a look at the body.”

CHAPTER THREE

The sun would be up soon, but the park was still shrouded in darkness. Hayden tossed her coffee cup in a nearby bin, and then followed the officer towards the crowd.

Hayden and Marcus stepped under the fluttering crime scene tape that cordoned off a grim tableau. As soon as she got there, the man with the mustache disappeared. He clearly didn't want to be too involved in the case.

The bench at the center of the investigation was an incongruous focal point among the tranquil surroundings. Uniformed officers, their faces etched with concern, patrolled the perimeter, ensuring the few late-night joggers kept their distance.

The local police officers looked at her and Marcus.

"Agent Smart," she announced crisply to the other officers, displaying her badge with a practiced flick of her wrist. Her eyes, keen and assessing, swept over the scene, cataloging every detail from the position of the bench to the disposition of the uniforms.

"Officer Gaines," the man responded, nodding toward her with a mixture of respect and relief. His weary gaze told of hours already spent at the scene. "Some kids found her around two in the morning—said they were just looking for a quiet spot after the bars closed."

"Anything you can tell us about the body?" Marcus inquired, his notebook already open, pen poised.

Gaines hesitated, his hand running through his short-cropped hair before gesturing vaguely towards the bench. "It's odd," he started, shifting uncomfortably. "The way she's sitting there... It's not normal. Doesn't seem like a simple overdose or heart attack. It's as if someone wanted to send a message, but we're damned if we know what it is."

"Thank you, Officer," Hayden said, her mind already ticking over the possibilities. Each case was a puzzle, and this one had just presented its first enigmatic piece.

There were too many others in the way for Hayden to get a good look, so she pushed her way through to the front of the crowd.

The sea of blue uniforms parted like curtains as Hayden approached the tape-enclosed bench. The early morning sun cast long shadows across the park, draping over the scene in a silent vigil. As she stepped into the cleared space, her gaze fell upon the woman on the bench.

Hayden's breath hitched, a cold finger tracing down her spine. Instinctively, one hand rose to cover her mouth, stifling the gasp that threatened to escape.

Words deserted her, the horror unfolding before her eyes rendering her momentarily mute.

No matter how many cases she worked, this moment never became any easier.

There, seated almost serenely on the weathered wooden slats, was the woman—head lolling gently to one side. Her hands lay folded atop the fabric of her shirt, resting over her stomach. Eyelids closed, she could have been mistaken for a statue, an eerie mimicry of tranquility in the bustling city park.

A glint of sunlight caught on a string of beads encircling the woman's neck—a discordant note of beauty amid the dark reality of the scene. But it was the vile trail of vomit streaking from the corner of her mouth, dribbling down her chin and darkening the wood beneath, that tore at Hayden's composure.

"Christ," she murmured under her breath, professionalism holding back the bile rising in her own throat.

It was a grotesque punctuation to the silent scream of the scene—the undeniable stamp of an unnatural death.

Hayden's eyes traced every detail, the seasoned detective in her cataloging the clues even as her humanity recoiled. She knew this dance with death all too well; each step, each turn, was a path towards the truth, no matter how twisted it became.

Hayden's gaze lingered on the grotesque trail leading from the woman's lips, a morbid river that spoke of silent agony.

She turned to Marcus, her voice steady despite the churn in her gut.

"That makes it almost certain. She was poisoned," she said, a grim certainty shading her words. "This isn't an accidental overdose or a heart attack. Look at her—no one ends up posed like that unless..."

"Unless what?" Marcus prompted, his own eyes scouring the scene, searching for the invisible threads that might stitch this mystery together.

"Unless they're trying to tell us something," Hayden replied, her mind sparking as synapses connected disparate memories.

"Something about this seems familiar," she said. "But I can't put my finger on what."

“Familiar how?” Marcus asked. He took a few pictures of the scene, to have as a redundancy in addition to those taken by the crime scene photographer who was already taking pictures of the scene.

“I don’t know,” she answered. She took a long look at the way Laura’s hands rested on her stomach, as if to make her look relaxed, content, or full.

And then there was the string of beads around her neck. The bright red beads looked cheap, as if from some dollar store, the type of jewelry that children use to add to their costumes. Given the rest of Laura’s yoga instructor outfit, Hayden doubted that she had purchased them herself.

But why would the killer place them on her? What did that tell them about his psychology?

"There was another case, remember? Naomi Cruz?"

Recognition flickered in Marcus's eyes. He nodded, stepping closer. "Was she the singer?"

“Actress,” Hayden corrected. “She was up and coming, had booked a few big roles.”

"Yeah, I remember. Found in her apartment with similar..." His voice trailed away as Hayden reached into her coat pocket.

Her fingers found the familiar coolness of her phone, and with a few swift taps, the screen lit up with the archived details of Naomi Cruz's unfortunate demise.

“She was poisoned too, but that could just be a coincidence,” he added.

“It isn’t the poison that concerns me,” she said. “It was the way the body was staged. In Naomi’s case, the killer left a piece of costume jewelry on her body too… an earring. He also placed a scarf around her head. The original detective on the case could never figure out why, and eventually it was labeled as cold.”

“And you think this is the same guy?”

“Could be.”

She knew that if she could see the picture, she would have a better time assessing if the cases were related.

It didn’t take long to log into a secure database and search for the file.

The picture of Naomi, lifeless on her living room floor with signs of a struggle absent, resonated with eerie similarity. There had been no vomit in Naomi's case, but there were telltale signs of poisoning and irritation around the mouth. They were unmistakably similar.

"Look at this," Hayden said, tilting the screen towards Marcus. Her thumb scrolled through the digital case file, past the testimonies and toxicology reports. "Arsenic in her system. It was subtle, almost missed by the coroner. If this" —she gestured back toward the bench where the latest victim sat— "isn't a coincidence, we could be looking at a serial scenario."

"Or a copycat," Marcus mused, his brow furrowing as he considered the possibilities.

"Either way," Hayden concluded, slipping her phone back into her pocket, "we've got a pattern. And patterns mean purpose. We just need to figure out what it is."

Marcus stepped back, head tilted as he observed the body from a different angle. "You know the way she's sitting feels strange." He gestured toward the woman, her hands resting almost peacefully on her abdomen. "It's simple, but it feels... intentional."

Hayden watched Marcus's analysis, her thoughts aligning with his observations. The staged serenity of the scene clashed with its inner horror, a dichotomy that nagged at her. As he spoke, an itch of familiarity scratched at the back of her mind, a memory just out of reach trying to surface.

"I know. There's something familiar about this, too. The way that the bright colors have been arranged," Hayden murmured, more to herself than to Marcus. There was something about the way the victim was positioned—a quietness in the arrangement that evoked a sense of déjà vu.

With the scene etched in her mind's eye, Hayden pulled a small, worn notepad from her jacket pocket along with a pencil. Flipping it open to a blank page, she began to sketch the sight before her.

The crisp air carried the scent of dew and the distant murmur of city life as she shaded in the outline of the bench, the slant of the victim's head, the unnatural stillness of her hands.

She had trained originally as a sketch artist. Her drawings based on witness descriptions had appeared all over the news, and they'd been used by law enforcement to track down dozens of criminals.

But eventually, she wanted to learn to solve cases herself, so she became an FBI agent.

Sometimes she missed the simple days as a sketch artist, where all she had to do was pay attention to the words of the people affected by cases, comfort them as she interpreted their descriptions. and work memories into a picture that they could see and touch.

She still found that it helped her to draw the scenes and suspects.

It forced her to focus on the small details around her, to slow her thinking so she could see things as they really were. But it also meant that she garnered a reputation around the field office for being a bit strange.

The scratch of graphite against paper was methodical, a rhythm that helped her focus. Each stroke felt like a step closer to understanding, a way to dissect the bizarre presentation layer by layer. She sketched with precision, capturing every detail—the beads around her neck, the grim line of her closed lips.

While other detectives preferred to take pictures, she drew the scene.

Eventually, she had the whole thing replicated on the page. She captured every detail, from the haunting look on Laura's face, to the park bench, to the placement of the tree branches in the background.

There was something strangely tranquil about the way it all looked, and the thought of that made her shudder.

She made quick notes to add to her initial sketch. She knew that she would want to look back on much of this later. The act of sketching forced her to confront the reality of death from all possible angles, both literal and metaphorical. With every line, she sought not just the what, but the why behind this morbid display.

Marcus watched over her shoulder, silent now, knowing that for Hayden this process was more than mere documentation—it was her pathway into the killer's mind. And with each detail committed to paper, they were one step closer to unraveling the mystery that had been so carefully laid out on a public park bench.

"Not much more we can do for her now," he said. "The coroner will take a look at her, and we'll get back to investigating first thing. Try to get a little sleep, okay?"

"You too," she said, but she knew that the image of Laura's blank face would keep her up for a long time.

CHAPTER FOUR

The morning sun had barely kissed the Seattle skyline as Hayden pushed through the revolving doors of the field office, her stride less energetic than it typically was. It was evident in the slight drooping of her shoulders and the way she ran a hand through her disheveled chestnut hair that the late hours were taking their toll.

She hadn't been home for long, just enough time to shower, eat a quick breakfast, and then leave again.

The city was waking up, but for Hayden, sleep was a distant memory clouded by visions of crime scenes and unanswered questions.

She made a beeline for the break room and made a fresh pot of coffee. She waited impatiently for the stuff to brew, and then she found her favorite mug in the cupboard, the one that was decorated with a series of paint brushes.

With a steaming cup clasped between her hands, the warmth seeped into her chilled skin, promising a semblance of revival. Clutching this small comfort, she navigated the maze of desks, each step steadier than the last, until she reached her own workspace—a chaotic testament to the many cases that had consumed her days and haunted her nights.

Her desk was an island in a sea of order, strewn with sketches that captured frozen moments of violence and mystery. She wasn't exactly known for being organized. She had to dig through piles of papers just to find a spot to put her coffee mug down.

On impulse, she smoothed out a crease in the sketch from last night's scene, her gaze lingering on the stark lines and shadows that detailed the final tableau of a life unjustly taken. It was an unwelcome addition to her collection, yet another puzzle demanding to be solved.

As she placed the drawing among its grim companions, the ping of an incoming email cut through the quiet hum of the office. Hayden tapped the keyboard of her computer, eyes scanning the digital missive with practiced efficiency.

For a moment, her mind was blank. There were no leads on the case yet. Where would she start?

She decided to check her email and found that she had a new message in her inbox: the coroner's report.

She opened the file and found more post-mortem pictures of Laura's body, showing the lack of external marks. There were also photos of the costume beads.

The coroner had noted that there was no evidence of the killer left behind, no fingerprints or strands of hair. The contents of her stomach had been empty, other than the poison, and there was no evidence of alcohol in her system. The coroner had checked for signs of foul play, sexual assault, and found none.

Hayden scrolled through the large section of the document explaining all the things that weren't there. Only some scarring around where the victim had been given chloroform to incapacitate her.

Then she found the place where the coroner had detailed the cause of death.

The report distilled the tragedy of the previous night into clinical facts and detached findings, but one line stood out stark and irrefutable. Cause of death: arsenic poisoning.

Due to bruising around her mouth and throat, the evidence suggested that she had been force-fed a large amount of arsenic after being knocked out.

A cold knot formed in the pit of Hayden's stomach. Poison—a silent, invisible killer that left its victims in unsuspecting agony.

With the official cause confirmed, the pieces of the puzzle began to shift, aligning into a more sinister picture that Hayden knew all too well. This wasn't just an isolated incident; it was a calculated act of malice. The challenge now was not only to find justice for the victim but to untangle the web of deceit woven by a murderer who remained shrouded in darkness.

But at the same time, arsenic seemed a strange, almost archaic choice.

Hayden's fingers drummed a staccato rhythm on the wooden surface of her desk, the sound punctuating the silence that enveloped her in the early morning office. Her mind was alight with the details of last night's crime scene, when an unsettling recollection took hold. Slowly, she slid open the bottom drawer where older case files were stashed away from prying eyes, their contents a catalogue of unsolved mysteries. She rifled through them, the manila folders whispering against one another, until she found the one that had been nagging at the edge of her consciousness.

"Naomi Cruz," she murmured, reading the blocky print on the tab. The file felt heavier than it looked as she placed it on her desk, its weight a testament to the unresolved questions it contained.

Flipping it open, she was greeted by the grainy monochrome of crime scene photos and the sparse notes of a case grown cold. Naomi, a young woman of 25, had been discovered in her house; arsenic had coursed through her veins, ushering her from life to death with cruel intention.

With her jaw set firm, Hayden focused on the images before her, the photographs capturing Naomi's final position.

Unlike the recent victim, Naomi had been laid out on the cold concrete floor, her body arranged with an eerie deliberateness. Her head had been turned at an unnatural angle, as if her lifeless eyes were forever searching over her shoulder, peering into a past that would never release its secrets.

The similarity of the arsenic poisoning was chilling enough, but it was the staging—the meticulous positioning of Naomi's body—that gnawed at Hayden's instincts.

Of course, there was also the plastic earring left in one ear. That was the part that Hayden simply couldn't ignore.

Hayden leaned back in her chair; her gaze locked on the pictures as she allowed the implications of these two deaths to wash over her. The connection was more than coincidence; it was a pattern, one she couldn't afford to overlook. With a resolute breath, she gathered the files, her mind churning with possibilities.

Whoever they were dealing with was not only lethal but also deliberate in their actions. And now, it was up to her to decipher the message left behind by a murderer who seemed to be speaking directly to them, albeit in a language written in poison and calculated displays of the dead.

The clatter of keys and the shuffle of feet marked the arrival of Marcus.

Hayden didn't need to look up to know her partner had entered the room; his presence carried a distinct energy that filled the space. He dropped his bag with a thud and settled into the desk beside hers, mirroring her weary posture.

"Morning, Hayden. You get any sleep?" Marcus ran a hand through his hair, the dark circles under his eyes betraying the formality of his question.

"Sleep's a luxury we can't afford right now," she replied without missing a beat, her voice tinged with the same exhaustion that weighed on her eyelids.

Marcus nodded in silent agreement, understanding all too well the toll their line of work took on them.

Hayden turned her chair to face him, the manila folder in her hands feeling like a leaden weight. She opened it, revealing the juxtaposition of photos and documents she'd been poring over since dawn.

"Take a look at this," she urged, sliding the folder across the small gap that separated their desks. "That's the rest of Naomi' Cruz's file. It's more detailed than what I was able to dig up last night. And I got the coroner's report. Laura was poisoned. Arsenic."

“What is this, the 1750s?” he asked.

“That’s what I thought. It’s a strange choice. Especially since it would be hard to get in its raw form these days.”

Marcus leaned in, his attention captured as he scanned the contents. The images showed the two young women, each death scene meticulously arranged by the killer's unseen hands. In one photo, Naomi lay on the ground, her head twisted unnaturally, eyes forever peering backward, a scarf tied around her head. Another depicted the recent victim, positioned with an unsettling grace that belied the violence of her end.

"Both victims were young women, poisoned, and both were found in staged crime scenes."

Hayden's finger traced the outline of the pictures as she spoke, her tone conveying the gravity of their predicament. "It's not just about killing for this person—it's theater."

Marcus met her gaze, the initial skepticism in his eyes giving way to a dawning realization. They shared a silent moment, the unspoken acknowledgment that they were likely hunting the same specter that had orchestrated these grim performances.

Marcus rubbed the stubble on his chin, a small furrow creasing his brow as he mulled over the information strewn before them.

“I think the same man committed both crimes,” she said. “And if we don’t stop him, I think he’ll kill again.”

"I'm just not convinced we're looking at a serial situation here, Hayden. The M.O. is bizarre, sure, but..."

"Look at the patterns, Marcus." Hayden's voice was steady, insistent. She leaned back in her chair, arms crossed, her eyes never leaving his. "It's too specific. The staging, the poison—it's like a signature."

"Or a weird coincidence," Marcus countered, though the conviction in his tone had begun to wane. "But without any DNA, no fibers, no prints... we're grasping at shadows."

"Well, we can't wait around for him to kill someone else before we get to work."

Marcus nodded slowly, conceding the point as his analytical mind began to turn over the possibilities. He leaned back against the cold metal of his chair, the cogs of his thoughts visibly turning.

"Okay, let's say you're right," he finally said. "Where do we begin?"

Hayden's gaze moved from Marcus to the towering stacks of paperwork and case files on her desk. Her hand reached out, fingers brushing past the sketches and reports until they paused on a photograph—a smiling family portrait that seemed so painfully normal. Laura, the most recent victim, beamed from the center, her life's potential cut tragically short.

"Her family," Hayden murmured, tapping the photo with a decisive motion. "If we can peel back the layers of Laura's life, maybe we'll find a thread to pull, a connection. We could figure out if she knew Naomi. Or, at the very least, we could find out if she had any enemies."

"Family dynamics, relationships, patterns of behavior..." Marcus mused, nodding in agreement. "You think the killer knew her personally?"

"Maybe," Hayden replied, pushing herself up from the desk with a renewed sense of purpose. "It's a place to start. Or there's a link we're missing, something that ties her to Naomi Cruz. We start with those closest to Laura; someone there might hold the key to unraveling this whole thing."

Together, they stood, united in their resolve, their exhaustion temporarily forgotten as they prepared to delve into the intricate tapestry of a life taken too soon. It was a grim task, but for Hayden and Marcus, it was the beacon in the dark, guiding them towards an elusive truth hidden within the heartache of loss.

CHAPTER FIVE

The tires of the unmarked police sedan crunched over the gravel as Hayden pulled up to the curb outside a sprawling suburban house. She killed the engine and sat for a moment, taking in the sight. Laura's sister lived comfortably, it seemed. The huge front yard was manicured with precision, blooming flower beds punctuating the green expanse like strokes of an artist's brush. The porch was an inviting array of potted plants and wicker furniture, a testament to a life that held at least the illusion of tranquility.

"Does she know?" Hayden asked. She hated to break the news to the families of victims. She always felt deeply for their loss, but at the same time, she could never find the right words to say.

"I think the Seattle PD contacted the family as soon as Laura's body was identified," said Marcus. "So, we're in the clear."

Hayden took a breath to steady herself. She had lost her own sister, and she knew what that felt like. She remembered when the police asked her a seemingly endless list of questions about the man who had taken her. What did he look like? Where were you? What were you doing?

All she had wanted to do that day was collapse, and cry.

She tried to push the memory of that day out of her mind. Losing her sister had cost her family everything, torn their dynamic apart.

She couldn't help but wonder if tragedy would do the same to Laura's family.

Hayden reached for the file, flipping it open to confirm the details she already knew by heart.

"Do you know anything about the sister?" she asked Marcus.

"I meant to look her up but didn't get a chance to."

"I had a chance to do a little research," Hayden told him. "Turns out she works for one of those big tech companies in town. I think that she does PR for them."

"Impressive," he said.

"I have no idea if they were close or not, but hopefully she knows something helpful."

Kelly, Laura's sister, had climbed the ranks at Synaptech, one of the big tech companies in the city. It was the kind of detail that could mean everything or nothing, but every thread had to be followed.

She stepped out of the car, the door closing with a soft thud behind her, and made her way up the walkway. Each step seemed to echo with the weight of the task before her. As she approached, the front door swung open, revealing a woman whose eyes were rimmed with red yet sparkled with a resilience that spoke volumes of her character.

"Hello," Hayden said. "We're sorry to disturb you. We're with the FBI and we're investigating your sister's case."

"I got a call that someone would come by with questions," she said, her voice holding a tremor that she couldn't quite disguise.

"I'm Agent Smart, and his is my partner, Agent Doyle. And we're here to help. I know how hard this is, but do you think you could answer a few questions for us?"

"Of course. Come inside," she said, stepping aside to welcome Hayden into the sanctuary of her home. Her smile was practiced, but underneath, the grief clung to her like a shadow. "Come in."

Hayden nodded, crossing the threshold while silently noting the effort Kelly made to present a composed demeanor. There was strength in her posture, a fortitude that came perhaps from years of navigating the male-dominated echelons of the tech world. Yet, despite the polished exterior, there was no mistaking the pain that lay just beneath the surface – the pain of a sister lost, whose absence turned even the most beautiful of homes into something incomplete.

Crossing the home's threshold, Hayden was immediately struck by the harmonious blend of technology and design. The foyer led to a living space where sunlight streamed through large windows, glinting off metallic surfaces and casting soft shadows across sleek, minimalist furniture. It was as if she had stepped into the pages of a high-end lifestyle magazine, one that celebrated the convergence of form and function.

She couldn't help but think about the contrast of her own living space, a messy clutter of sketches, used furniture, and cat hair.

Hayden was almost afraid to touch anything for fear that she'd make a mess.

"What do you do for work? I saw in my research that you work for Synaptech?"

"Oh, it's very boring. You probably wouldn't be interested to hear about that. I help with the ROI of our branding and storytelling department, utilizing spend, organic, and other kinds of ads to better…" she could tell by the look on their faces that she'd lost them.

"Marketing. I'm talking about marketing."

"Oh. Okay." Hayden couldn't deny that she was completely lost but decided to move on.

"Please, have a seat," Kelly offered, gesturing towards a sculptural white couch that seemed too pristine for comfort. Yet, when Hayden and Marcus settled onto its cushions, they found it surprisingly accommodating.

"Thank you," Hayden began, her eyes briefly scanning the room. a symphony of smart devices were seamlessly integrated into the decor. It was clear that Kelly's professional life was mirrored in her personal space, efficiency and innovation within arm's reach without sacrificing aesthetic appeal.

"Kelly, we understand this is a difficult time for you," Hayden said with genuine empathy, "but anything you can tell us about Laura's life could be helpful."

Kelly's eyes softened at the mention of her sister, and she took a moment before responding. "Laura... she was someone who lived with intention. She wasn't just a yoga instructor; she embodied the practice. To her, it was more than exercise—it was a philosophy for living. She went through a rough patch, and it really helped her get back on track."

"What kind of rough patch?"

"I mean, what kind is there? Her boyfriend broke up with her, she started drinking heavily. I think she sort of hit rock bottom."

"And you said that she was passionate?" Hayden probed gently.

"Absolutely," Kelly affirmed. "She dedicated her life to yoga, constantly learning and teaching others. You could say she'd found her calling—helping people find balance and peace in their lives."

A slight quiver in Kelly's voice betrayed the sorrow of loss, but her pride in Laura's achievements was unmistakable.

Hayden noticed how Kelly's hands unconsciously traced the lines of an invisible yoga pose, a physical echo of her words. It was a small, telling detail that spoke volumes about the bond between the sisters—one grounded in mutual respect for each other's chosen paths.

"Would you say she spent most of her time at the yoga studio?"

"Yes. She led workshops almost every weekend, along with her regular classes. Of course, we got dinner once a week."

"What else can you tell us about her daily routine?" asked Marcus.

"I don't know. My work keeps me pretty busy. I think she liked to go for walks downtown."

Kelly's gaze wandered past the array of smart gadgets, pausing on a framed photograph of Laura in a poised asana, sunlight filtering through her hair. The silence seemed to stretch, filled only by the faint hum of technology at rest.

"Yoga was her world," Kelly continued, voice tinged with a mixture of admiration and something more elusive—perhaps a hint of envy or unspoken skepticism. "I'll be honest; I didn't always get it—the fascination with all the poses and mantras. I mean, I work in tech; our worlds couldn't be more different. But that was Laura... committed, no matter what anyone else thought. She loved it, and that love touched everyone she taught."

Hayden nodded, her mind cataloging each inflection in Kelly's voice, each flicker of emotion across her face.

"And does the name Naomi Cruz mean anything to you?"

"Naomi?" said Kelly. "I don't know. I don't think so. It might be a little familiar, but no one that she was close to."

"And you can't think of anyone who might have wanted to harm her? Maybe someone from one of her classes? Or someone from her tumultuous past?"

"None," Kelly said, firmly shaking her head, eyes clouding over. "It was more personal turmoil than relational turmoil. And her students loved her. She was one of the good ones. Who would want to kill someone who spent their life spreading peace?"

"Had she picked up any new hobbies recently?" asked Marcus. "Or did she change her routine in any way?"

"I wish I knew. She was always up to something, but I don't know the details. I'm sorry."

Hayden stood up slowly from the couch, her hands resting momentarily on the cool, white fabric. The question lingered in the air like an unresolved chord. As they made their way to the door, Hayden turned to look back at Kelly, who remained seated, lost in a sea of grief and incomprehension.

"Thank you for your time, Kelly. We'll do everything we can," Hayden assured her before stepping out into the daylight.

As the door closed behind them, Hayden felt the weight of the unsolved case pressing down. Laura's profession as a yoga instructor was a piece of the puzzle, but how it fit into the larger picture was still unclear. She walked down the meticulously kept path, mind turning over the possibilities. Was there a connection within Laura's classes? A disgruntled student? Or was it something more personal?

"Thinking about the yoga angle?" Marcus asked, his voice pulling her from her thoughts.

"Yeah," Hayden replied, her stride purposeful. "It feels significant, but I'm not sure why. There's a piece we're missing, and it's bothering me."

"Let's go over what we have so far," Marcus suggested as they reached the car. Hayden nodded in agreement, her detective instincts telling her that the answer was there, somewhere tangled in the threads of a peaceful practice and a violent end.

***

Hayden's heels clicked against the sterile linoleum floor, a staccato rhythm that matched the quickening pulse of her investigation. The field office was a hive of activity, detectives hunched over desks, their conversations a low hum of theories and leads. Marcus was already there, his eyes buried in the glow of a computer screen as he scrolled through endless lines of research.

"Anything?" she asked, keeping her tone neutral despite the urgency bubbling inside her.

"Still digging," was Marcus's terse reply, his focus unwavering.

Nodding, Hayden turned away, feeling the tug of intuition guiding her towards another approach. She found solace in the quietude of an empty conference room; its large table was an untouched canvas waiting for her to piece together a mosaic of crime scenes that whispered secrets in silence.

She laid out the printed pictures, a grim gallery of still life where each captured the essence of chaos frozen in time. She pulled out each of her sketches of the previous crime scene and studied the images, looking for something that she had missed.

She familiarized herself with what she already knew about the scene, seeing nothing that she'd missed before.

Something nagged at the edges of her consciousness, a pattern that played hide and seek within the graphite lines. Hayden leaned back in her chair, her gaze darting between her drawings and the photographs, searching for the elusive thread that connected them.

"Come on, what are you trying to tell me?" she murmured under her breath, a mantra for clarity.

The room's fluorescent light buzzed overhead, casting a clinical glow over her workspace. She reached for another sheet, starting afresh, her strokes growing more determined. The familiarity was there, a ghostly presence that hovered just out of reach, taunting her with its significance. Hayden knew it held the key, a silent witness to a truth yet unveiled, and she would coax it into the light, one line at a time.

CHAPTER SIX

That same day, in the sterile silence of an almost empty studio, a man was perched on the edge of a solitary mattress, its corners frayed, and the fabric tinged with the dust of disuse.

The stark white walls, unadorned and grim, bore witness to the room's nakedness, save for the small kitchenette whose surfaces gleamed under the harsh fluorescent light. A few buckets, their vibrant contents long since dried into crumbled memories of color, stood as forgotten sentinels amid the desolation.

The windows were plastered over with butcher paper to keep the light away. He found that it distracted him from his work. He liked it better when it was difficult to tell what time of day it was. In college, he had paid for a studio with no natural light so he could work all day or night without worrying about silly constructs like time.

He was tired. He tried to remember the last time he had eaten something, and an empty feeling in his stomach told him that it had been a while. Still, he didn't seem to have time for simple things like buying or cooking food. His mind was far too busy for something like that.

He reached out, his fingers calloused and stained with the ghosts of paint, and swiped at the phone that lay beside him, it's screen a shard of light in the dimness. With deliberate swipes, he cycled through photographs captured not by an artist's loving eye but with a cold precision that belied the nature of their subject. They were not of sunset horizons or the curve of a still life; instead, they were candid snapshots of a woman named Erica Stanton.

Erica's image flickered across the digital canvas—her steps confident and her gaze fixed forward.

Each photo was a moment frozen, a slice of daily life, yet nothing about them spoke of the mundane or the innocent.

He knew that the quality of his camera didn't produce the best images. She appeared in a grainy resolution. This photo wouldn't be ready to show others any time soon, but then again, that wasn't the point. He had to remind himself that he was still in the research portion of the work.

The man studied her face, the way her hair fell in a practical style befitting someone who served the public without fanfare or expectation of glory. He zoomed in on one picture, where the sunlight threw half her features into shadow, casting her expression into something enigmatic and unknowable.

Her name seemed to echo against the barren walls, a name that filled the space and settled in the air like a tangible thing.

"Erica Stanton," he murmured, tasting the syllables as if they were a spell or invocation. Her role, her purpose in the community—defender of the voiceless, advocate for the forgotten—all played into the narrative he constructed around her, a narrative that was far from finished.

As he pocketed the phone, the man let the shadows reclaim the corner where the mattress lay, leaving only the faintest hint of light to outline his form—a specter in his own residence, preparing for what would come next.

He thought about earlier that morning, how he had easily followed her movements without her noticing his presence there. After all, he had faded into the background of the world rather quickly, forgotten by the very people who had once celebrated him. He could see it clearly now.

He had watched as Erica emerged from her apartment, her stride purposeful and her suit immaculate. With the casual focus of a seasoned tracker, he followed at a safe distance. She put her dog into her car, and he noted the absentminded way she scratched behind her dog's ears before dropping him off at daycare, a tender act contradicting her austere profession.

He always wondered what people would want a dog for, especially if they had no time to take care of it themselves.

Then he followed her farther to the tennis courts where she met with peers whose laughter rang out like peals of normalcy, none the wiser to the watchful eyes that traced their every movement. He listened to the sound of the yellow tennis balls bounce back and forth.

It was all so pristine, with the green grass, the white tennis skirts, the birds chirping in trees above.

As he lurked behind the chain-link boundaries of the court, his mind wandered to a different time, a different space.

Even if she didn't remember him, he remembered her.

He imagined Erica as she might have been through his artist's lens: poised, dignified, the perfect subject for a portrait that could hang in the hallowed halls of galleries and museums. Once, he might have approached her with a proposition, brushed oils onto canvas in an attempt to capture the essence of her being.

Not many people had a talent for modeling, but she had such a unique and striking face, with her sharp cheekbones, upturned nose, and arched eyebrows. Not to mention the proportions of her legs, the slope of her shoulders. She looked like a walking painting. Perfect in every way.

Now, the art he envisioned was of a different kind, entirely darker, more profound, not meant for the public eye but for the depths of his own understanding. It was an art born of compulsion, a testament to the intricate dance between predator and prey, observer and observed. In contemplating this clandestine masterpiece, he felt a twisted kinship with the very essence of creation, as if he were about to unveil the most significant work of his existence, painted in shadows and secrecy instead of vibrant hues.

He had come back to his studio, ready for the final steps of his plan.

The man's fingers trembled with a familiar anticipation as they reached for the weathered mask hanging on a nail by the door, its filters clogged with the relics of many toxic creations. He placed it over his face, the rubber sealing against his skin, the scent of old paint and turpentine faint but comforting.

His studio, once vibrant with splashes of color, now served as the staging ground for a different kind of craft. He turned to the small kitchenette, where two innocuous bottles sat side by side on the counter — one held vinegar, the other bleach. In another life, these were mere household cleaners, but in his hands, they were the components of something far more insidious.

With the precision of a seasoned artist mixing his palette, he combined the liquids in a deliberate ratio, the chemical reaction beginning immediately.

The clear solution gave way to a sinister chlorine scent, indicative of the transformation into chloroform.

The concoction was simple, yet effective: a tool to silence and subdue.

He was careful not to get too close, should he accidentally poison himself. It had taken him a few days to get the ratio right, but now he had the perfect system.

He moved methodically, the way he used to when preparing his canvas, only now there was no canvas, just the impending void where his subject would momentarily exist. From a high shelf, he retrieved an unassuming container labeled with a skull and crossbones – arsenic, the king of poisons, once a staple in the artist's arsenal for pigments vibrant and deadly alike.

It was the perfect instrument. The only problem was getting the women to ingest it. That was what the chloroform was for. First, he incapacitated them; then he could easily force the poison down their throats.

He took a pinch of the powdered toxin, its fine grains like the dust of crushed bones, and wrapped it carefully in a small sachet of paper. This was his nod to the past, a tribute to the days when art was synonymous with danger, when beauty could be lethal.

In the dim light of the studio, he tucked the bag into his pocket, feeling its weight as both a burden and a necessity. It was a grim reminder of the path he had chosen, a road paved not with the bright oils of yesteryear but with the dark promise of an act that whispered of finality.

Tonight, he was not an artist of canvases and paint but an orchestrator of fate, wielding tools of silence and swift demise, preparing to capture his subject in a tableau that would never be shared. Yet somehow it felt like his most significant piece to date.

Staring into the abyss of his own calculated intent, he paced the perimeter of the studio. Each step was a silent rehearsal, a ghostly pantomime of the abduction to come. The room felt colder now, stripped of its former identity as a sanctuary for creation, now a staging ground for predation.

He visualized the sequence: a quick approach, a firm hand over Erica Stanton's mouth, the soaked rag with its noxious fumes rendering her unconscious. The image was disturbingly crisp in his mind; there would be no hesitation when the moment arrived.

He would need to be a shadow, an unperceived blip in the periphery of the public eye.

Every motion must be fluid, every choice precise. The margin for error was nonexistent, but he had a steady hand. And more important than that, he had a better vision.

Like a tryptic, she could become his third in a grand series of work.

He had studied her routines, knew the moments she was most vulnerable, and understood that the slightest miscalculation could unravel everything. In his mind's eye, he saw himself moving with the precision of a panther, every muscle coiled and ready to pounce at the ordained time.

A sense of purpose fortified him as he surveyed the stark room once again—his haven from the world's prying eyes. His actions, though dark, were a form of expression that transcended the mundane strokes of a brush on canvas. This was his art now, one that required a different palette, tools forged from shadows and silence.

The police might scour the city for him, but this barren place, this temporary abode of his twisted muse, sat beyond suspicion's reach.

No one was looking for him. Not here.

It was a nondescript fortress, invisible to all who lacked the imagination to see it as anything more than a hollow chamber.

With a breath that seemed to draw in the very darkness around him, he gathered his macabre ensemble.

The chloroform, tightly sealed; the arsenic in a small bag, discreetly pocketed; and the mask that helped him protect himself and hide his identity, an old friend, once worn to guard against the toxic fumes of oil paints, now repurposed as a shield for a far more sinister artistry.

As he stood in the center of the now-transformed studio, the air hung heavy with anticipation. In his mind, each item was an instrument, each step a stroke, and the night ahead was a canvas awaiting his indelible mark. With hands that were steady and resolute, he collected his supplies, the weight of his resolve grounding him to the earth beneath his feet.

He was ready to create his next masterpiece, a piece so profound in its silence that it would never be seen yet would define him forever. Tonight, he would capture something eternal, not through pigment, but through the act of an artist who had stepped beyond the edge of sanity into a realm where life itself was his medium.

CHAPTER SEVEN

The graphite tip of Hayden's pencil skittered across the paper, a frenetic ballet of lines and shadows that revealed an almost supernatural recreation of the crime scenes. Paper canvases littered the conference room table and spilled onto the floor around her, each one a window into the moments of horror she was trying to unravel.

Back inside her secluded conference room, she had taken over the space with more sketches and notes from each scene.

This one looked like all the others, with a round table at the center, perfect for spreading out her various drawings. She looked back and realized that she had drawn the same angles of one scene half a dozen times. Next to that were her own sketches of the costume jewelry.

She had gotten to the point where she wasn't even thinking about the case, just about the way that she had captured the faces of the victims. She found the shape of Laura's nose particularly difficult to capture. It was the same with the angle at which Naomi's neck was turned, with her gaze pointed over her shoulder, the scarf tied around her head.

Hayden thought about the time and care it would have taken to put these victims in the exact positions that they were in.

She remembered the comment about chloroform, and wondered why the killer would go to the length to poison them when a high enough dosage of chloroform would have done the job. It was almost as if he tried to poison them twice.

She leaned back in her chair, scrutinizing the latest sketch—the angle of a fallen face, the sprawl of a lifeless hand—before diving back in to adjust a line, deepen a contour.

Usually, she saw something new by now.

She waited for something to jump out. A twig out of place, a piece of clothing that didn't fit, a shape or number. Anything that could point her towards the killer.

She had an excellent visual memory, and the process of drawing helped her notice things that she had missed before. Of course, because of the time of Naomi's death, when it came to her case, she had to rely on pictures instead of firsthand knowledge.

She stood up from her chair and took a step back.

How much money did she cost the department in sketch paper alone?

The door creaked open, and Marcus stepped inside, his brow furrowing as he took in the eerie gallery that had consumed the room. "Hayden," he began, his voice tinged with a hint of unease, "this is... intense."

Without looking up, Hayden swapped pencils for a softer lead, shading in a dark pool that represented congealed blood.

"It needs to be," she replied, her hand never pausing. "It's all in the details."

Marcus circled the room, trailing his fingers over the back of an empty chair, his gaze locked on the papers that seemed to pulsate with silent screams and whispered secrets. He stopped behind Hayden, peering over her shoulder at the newest addition to her collection.

"Doesn't it get to you?" he asked quietly, the images reflected in his eyes. "Living these scenes over and over?"

She pressed her lips together. Sometimes Hayden felt like she lived in a crime scene— she had enough of them pinned to her wall. And if she was being honest with herself, it did get to her. She slept uneasily, and constantly felt on edge, as though someone was watching her, waiting for her to fail.

"Has to be done," Hayden said curtly, her focus unbreakable. Her fingers smudged a shadow into place, breathing life into the macabre stillness of the drawing before her. "I'm close to something. I can feel it."

Marcus nodded slowly, though the chill of realization still danced up his spine. The dedication in Hayden's pursuit bordered on obsession, but he understood the drive, the need for answers. In every stroke, every recreated drop of blood and broken expression, he saw not only the echo of tragedy but the relentless determination of the woman who would stop at nothing to piece together the fractured truth hidden within.

Hayden's hand moved with a deftness that belied the gravity of her task, each line a silent testament to a life she once envisioned.

"I wanted to be an artist," she murmured, almost to herself, as if the confession could seep into the paper and lighten the weight of the darkness she sketched.

Marcus paused, his eyes lifting from the grim tableaux to the woman before him. "An artist? You never told me that."

"Uh-huh." She drew a breath, her pencil hovering momentarily. "When I was a kid, I dreamed of going to art school. Almost applied."

The words hung between them, fragile and ghost-like. "But then... my sister vanished. Everything changed. Things turned out differently."

"You were the best sketch artist I've ever worked with, so your skills are put to good use here," he said.

She nodded. "Thanks."

"Drawing these..." Marcus began, gesturing to the room ensnared in graphite echoes.

"Helps me see," Hayden finished for him, the pencil resuming its dance across the pad. "Not just the crimes—it's like I can touch the truth, however ugly it may be."

Silence settled back over the room with only the scratch of Hayden's pencil filling the void. Marcus watched her a moment longer, the raw edge of her talent on full display, a poignant reminder of paths rerouted by unforeseen sorrow.

"Speaking of truth," he said after a heavy pause, breaking the near reverent stillness. "I've been digging into the coworkers at the yoga studio. Not that any of them are the type, but they all have alibis for the night of the murder."

"Figures," she replied without surprise, the lines under her fingers growing sharper, more insistent. "Did any of them give other details about her life?"

"She was universally liked by her students. She was sort of new to the studio, but fit right in. We'll keep looking," Marcus affirmed, his resolve matching the intensity of her strokes.

"Exactly." Hayden added a final shadow to her drawing, sealing the fate of paper to memory. "We keep looking until the picture is complete."

Hayden leaned in, her eyes narrowing as she scrutinized the images she had sketched with such fervent detail. Each line, each shadow on the paper brought her closer to an understanding that seemed to dance just beyond reach. There was a message here, in the tilt of a head, the sprawl of limbs—something painfully familiar. She exhaled slowly, her gaze not leaving the sketches as if she could will them to yield their secrets.

"Any ideas?" Marcus's voice was low, almost hesitant, respectful of the sanctuary of thought Hayden had enveloped herself within.

"Shh," she said softly, more to herself than to him, her mind churning. "There's something... I've seen this before."

Her voice was a whisper lost in the vast expanse of possibilities that lay within the graphite contours before her.

The room was silent again, save for the soft ticking of a clock on the wall, marking time in a world where time had stopped for two souls. And then it came to her, a rush of chilling clarity that made her heart skip a beat.

"Marcus," Hayden breathed, her finger hovering just above the paper, tracing an invisible line from one drawing to another. "I knew this was familiar. Look at them—their poses."

She didn't have to say more; the revelation etched on her face spoke volumes. It was there, in the artful arrangement of lifeless forms, a perverse homage hidden in plain sight. Both women, captured in death, were echoes of canvases laden with history, their final moments an imitation of immortal masterpieces.

Marcus furrowed his brow, clearly at a loss as he watched Hayden's finger dance in the air between the two drawings. "I don't get it," he said, his voice tinged with frustration.

"Think about it, Marcus," Hayden urged, stepping closer to the sketches of Laura. Her hand moved with deliberate strokes as she outlined the woman's repose. "The tilt of her head, the angle of her arm—it's not random. She's posed just like the woman in that Picasso painting. Ugh, what's it called?"

"You're looking at me like I know the answer," he said.

She pivoted toward the second set of drawings. Marcus followed, his gaze sharpening as he tried to catch up with her thoughts.

"And Naomi, look here." She framed an imaginary box around Naomi's face with her fingers. "Forget the ground beneath her, picture her upright, in a frame. What does this remind you of?"

Marcus hesitated, but the cloud of confusion began to lift from his eyes. Recognition dawned on him, slowly at first, then all at once.

"I guess... no, you've still lost me. I have no idea what you're getting at." He trailed off, unwilling to believe the conclusion that was forming in his mind.

"Paintings!" Hayden confirmed, her voice steady with certainty. "Laura has been posed to look like 'The Dream' by Picasso, right down to the string of beads around her neck."

"Was he the guy with the melting clocks?"

"No, that was Salvador Dalí."

"So, you're talking about the guy who did the one with the stars?"

She raised an eyebrow. “You can’t tell me you’ve never heard of Picasso?”

“I mean, I’ve heard of him, but…”

“When this case is over, I’m taking you to an art museum,” she said.

“Great,” he said, trying unsuccessfully to hide his lack of interest in art.

“One of his paintings depicts a woman in the exact pose that Laura was found. Hands on her stomach, head tilted to one side It’s called ‘The Dream.’ And in the painting, she’s wearing a string of beads, and her eyes are closed.”

“Oh…that’s interesting,” he put a hand to his chin, considering the implications.

“And Naomi—she’s like Vermeer's 'Girl with a Pearl Earring.' Just imagine a frame around her face."

“I’ve heard of that one,” he said. “But I can’t say I can picture it…”

“Well, you’ll have to trust me,” she said. “I took a trip to the Netherlands a few years back and saw it in person. I can’t believe I didn’t see it sooner.”

For a moment, they stood in silence, the weight of the revelation pressing down on them. Marcus stepped back, looking at the scenes anew, seeing beyond the gruesome details to the alarming pattern that had emerged.

"Art," he said finally, the word hanging between them, a key unlocking the twisted psyche of their suspect.

"Art," Hayden echoed, nodding solemnly. A sense of purpose ignited within her, a drive to unravel the mystery through the lens of her long-abandoned passion.

“So, our guy is setting up his crime scenes to imitate paintings?”

“It would seem so,” she answered.

“That’s unique.”

“I know,” she said. “I don’t understand. It’s a strange choice, to say the least. But that would explain why he goes out of his way to use arsenic.”

“How so?”

“They used to use it to make paint. It’s another reference to the art world.”

"Let's dive into the art world, see what connections we can find," Marcus suggested, already reaching for his phone to start the research.

"Agreed," Hayden replied, her eyes never leaving the sketches. They were more than just crime scenes now; they were a gallery of clues waiting to be interpreted, and she was determined to decode every brushstroke.

CHAPTER EIGHT

Hayden's fingers paused mid-tap over her laptop's keyboard, the glow of the screen casting a spectral light on her furrowed brow. The crime scene photos lay strewn across the desk, each one showcasing an eerie mimicry of classical artwork that had long since been etched into the fabric of art history. The brushstrokes of violence mirrored the finesse of oil on canvas, sending a shiver down her spine.

She had also pulled up a few photos of "The Dream" and "Girl with a Pearl Earring," just for Marcus's reference.

"Those are actually pretty good," he mused. "But I guess when it comes to art, 'Dogs Playing Poker' is about the extent of my knowledge."

"You have got to be joking," she said.

"Let's just say I'm glad you noticed the connection. I see it now, but I never would have found it for myself."

She also pulled up "The Persistence of Memory" by Dalí, just for good measure.

"This is the one that you were talking about before. He's credited with being one of the first major surrealists, and I think that his use of space here is just excellent. Of course, if you wanted to look at what you expertly called 'the star painting' by Van Gogh…"

"As much as I'd love an art history class," he began, "I think that we should focus on the case."

"You're right." She closed out of the reference pictures and returned to looking at the case file.

"An artist," she murmured to herself, "there has to be an artist tangled up in this mess. Interesting that he used different paintings from different time periods. And the Picasso is one of his more obscure paintings. It's no 'old guitarist.'"

"I'm going to pretend that means something to me and move on," he said.

Marcus shifted in his chair opposite her, his eyes narrowing as he followed her train of thought. His mind had been wading through the murky waters of criminal profiles and potential suspects, but Hayden's intuition often cut through the fog with precision.

"Actually," Marcus began, the cogs visibly turning behind his analytical gaze, "if we're looking for someone who knows painting, I stumbled upon something earlier."

He swiped through his tablet until he found the information he'd bookmarked.

"When I got to a dead end with Laura's coworkers, I started looking into her students. And I found something. Miles Fletcher, local art critic—revered in some circles, reviled in others. It turns out he was once under the tutelage of Laura Henley. I didn't think much of it, but he'd have a knowledge of the paintings."

Hayden's head snapped up, her detective's instinct flaring to life at the mention of Henley, one of the victims whose past had proven as elusive as the shadows at dusk.

"This is great!" said Hayden, unable to hide her excitement. "That's our first solid lead connecting the art world directly to the victims. Maybe something went down between him and Laura. Some kind of conflict."

"Seems like it," Marcus agreed, his voice carrying a note of cautious optimism. "His perspective on Henley might just untangle some of these knots."

"Then we pay Mr. Fletcher a visit," Hayden stated, her resolve hardening like plaster setting into form. She closed her laptop with a definitive click, the action symbolic of her readiness to step away from theories and dive back into the tangible world where answers awaited them.

"Agreed," Marcus nodded, already standing, his movements efficient and purposeful.

They got to the car, and Hayden spent most of the ride talking about her favorite paintings.

"Are you sure I need to know all of this?"

The engine hummed softly as Hayden maneuvered the unmarked sedan through the labyrinth of city streets, the GPS directing them to Miles Fletcher's latest gallery. The mid-afternoon sun cast long shadows across Marcus's face, giving his features a stark contrast that seemed fitting for their mission. Hayden's fingers tightened on the steering wheel, her mind churning with anticipation.

"You never know," she said.

He leaned his head back on the seat.

"Here's hoping Fletcher sheds some light on this," she murmured.

Marcus glanced over, his eyes steady and reassuring.

The address led them to an up-and-coming district where art and commerce blended seamlessly. The gallery stood out among the boutique coffee shops and vintage bookstores, its facade a tapestry of glass and steel designed to draw the eye.

Hayden parked the car, and they stepped out into the cool embrace of the afternoon. She straightened her jacket, the fabric whispering against itself, and followed Marcus to the entrance of the gallery. Her heartbeat quickened—a cocktail of professional excitement and the aesthetic appreciation in which she seldom had time to indulge.

She had been out of the art world for some time, and wasn't familiar with Fletcher's criticism or galleries.

The door chimed their arrival, and the interior of the gallery unfolded before them like a secret world. High ceilings crowned the space, and spotlights punctuated the ambiance, each beam a sentinel guarding the art beneath.

Hayden's gaze swept across the room, settling on the paintings adorning the walls—each one a riot of color and form, speaking silent volumes. But it was the painting that resembled the ocean which stole her breath. It was as if the artist had captured the very essence of the sea, its vastness and depth rendered in hues of cerulean and foam.

"I guess this isn't so bad," Marcus remarked quietly, noting Hayden's fixation.

She raised an eyebrow at him.

"Okay, fine. It's beautiful," he said. "Is that what you want me to say?"

"Captivating," she agreed, her voice distant as the tide depicted in the painting. For a moment, just a fleeting second, the case receded from her thoughts, replaced by the raw emotion conveyed on canvas. It was a poignant reminder that amid the chaos of their investigation, beauty still found a way to the surface.

"Let's find Fletcher," Hayden said at last, reluctantly tearing her eyes away from the artwork. She stepped further into the gallery, her senses sharpened, ready to peel back the layers of mystery that Fletcher might be concealing.

Together, they moved deeper into the gallery, the weight of unspoken questions heavy in the air between them.

The echo of their footsteps blended with the hushed murmurs of gallery patrons as Hayden and Marcus navigated between islands of sculptures and walls lined with vivid artistry. As they moved, a figure detached itself from the shadow of an angular installation—a man with the casual elegance of someone who not only appreciated art but lived it.

Miles Fletcher approached with an easy smile, his eyes appraising them as if trying to discern their taste in art.

"Good afternoon," he greeted, extending a hand not yet offered. "I don't believe we've met. Are you looking for something particular? Perhaps the piece that caught your eye upon entry?"

"Actually," Marcus began, his tone professional, devoid of any inclination towards the art, "we're not here to buy."

“Well,” said Miles, with a slippery sweet voice. “No one ever is. But you never know when a painting will just demand that you can’t leave without it.”

Hayden watched Fletcher's brow arch slightly, curiosity lighting his features. She stepped forward, her FBI badge discreetly presented.

"We're with the FBI, Mr. Fletcher," she said, her voice steady. "We need to ask you some questions regarding—"

"Federal Bureau?" he interrupted, his demeanor transforming as though a switch had been flipped. The affable host was gone, replaced by a man suddenly on edge.

His voice lowered, tinged with a hint of alarm. "I'd have to ask you to leave. Now."

"Mr. Fletcher—" Hayden tried again.

"Please," he cut in, a note of urgency creeping into his voice. "Your presence is not good for business. My clients value their privacy and discretion.”

Hayden looked around. The gallery was mostly empty at that time of day. And she doubted that many criminals spent their time in private art galleries.

“Law enforcement presence will cause unnecessary distress," he said.

"Your cooperation is important," Marcus interjected, his tone firmer now, but Fletcher was already glancing past them, his expression tight.

“We know that this isn’t convenient,” said Hayden, “But we need to ask you a few questions about a case that we’re working.”

"Nothing to do with the case, nothing at all," Fletcher reiterated, gesturing towards the exit with a hand that betrayed the slightest tremor.

“You answered that one fairly quickly,” she observed.

“I am sorry, agents,” he hissed. “But this space is for buyers only. I don’t have time to waste. So, if you’d kindly purchase something, or leave.”

This made Hayden even more suspicious. Moments ago, he was ready to convince them to stay longer without the intention of buying anything.

"You'll have to take this elsewhere. This gallery is a sanctuary for art lovers, not a backdrop for criminal investigations."

Hayden exchanged a look with Marcus, a silent communication passing between them. They were stirring the waters here, provoking ripples they couldn't yet predict. But one thing was certain: Miles Fletcher was more than just a purveyor of beautiful canvases.

Hayden stepped forward, her FBI badge a glint of authority in the soft gallery lighting. "Mr. Fletcher," she began, her tone leaving no room for further evasion, "this isn't a request we can walk away from. The case we're investigating is of significant importance and your name has come up in connection with it. We need you to come with us for questioning."

Fletcher's eyes scanned their faces, calculating, as if trying to find an escape in their stern expressions. He edged back slightly, his hand grazing the frame of a nearby painting—an unconscious action linking him to the artwork surrounding them.

"Questioning?" he echoed, a hint of incredulity in his voice. "I've done nothing wrong. I won't be dragged out in front of my patrons. It would ruin me. I’d be the talk of the town."

“All publicity is good publicity?” said Hayden.

“Not in my line of work.”

"Then let's make this easy," Marcus chimed in, his posture rigid, every inch the federal agent ready to enforce the law. "No scene, just cooperation."

"Absolutely not." Fletcher's refusal was sharp, a clear challenge to their authority.

Marcus's gaze hardened. He took a step closer, closing the distance between them. His hand rested on the cuffs at his belt—a subtle but unmistakable threat. "If you don't come now, we'll be forced to arrest you. Obstruction of an official investigation is a serious offense, Mr. Fletcher. We can do this here or downtown, but either way, you're coming with us."

The standoff hung between them, charged with unspoken threats. Finally, Fletcher's shoulders slumped, resignation etching lines into his previously composed features. "Fine," he spat out, his voice barely above a whisper. With a last glance at the vibrant seascapes that seemed to mock the current tension, he moved past Hayden and headed towards the back room to gather his things.

Hayden exhaled quietly, sharing a brief nod with Marcus. They had their lead, and now it was time to pull at the thread Fletcher represented, unraveling the mystery one interview at a time.

CHAPTER NINE

Hayden's gaze fixed on Miles through the glass partition that separated the interrogation room from the rest of the world. The way he had dismissed her earlier, with a slight curl of his lip when she expressed more curiosity than capital, still stung. This new space was a far cry from his typical habitat.

She might have found it easier to go to art school if it weren't for pompous jerks like him, who thought that they owned good taste and used manipulative tactics to ensure that the paintings in their galleries remained priced at the highest possible number.

She couldn't let her personal feelings about Miles and people like him get in the way of the investigation, however.

Hayden reminded herself to remain objective. Ask questions. Follow the evidence. Only then could she find the truth and be confident about the conclusions to which it led.

"Ready?" Marcus murmured beside her, grounding her in the mission at hand.

Even if he didn't show it, she could tell that he was annoyed as well.

"Let's do this," Hayden replied, steeling herself as she pushed open the door.

The chime above announced their entrance, prompting Miles to turn with a practiced smile that didn't quite reach his eyes. He seemed to appraise them anew, perhaps trying to reconcile their previous non-buyer status with their current determined approach.

"Detectives. Decided that I've stewed for long enough?" Miles quipped, his voice smooth like velvet but with a barb hidden within its folds. "Which tactic will it be today? Good cop, bad cop?"

"This isn't television," Hayden began, stepping forward so that the barrier no longer stood between them, "We have actual investigative work to do, and we would appreciate your cooperation."

"Please," he said. "I have nothing to hide. Ask all the questions that you should choose."

Hayden gave a fake smile. "I'm curious about your story. How did you find yourself in the gallery business?"

Miles paused, the question seeming to take him by surprise. “What is this, an exposé on the secrets of my success?” His mask of sophistication flickered, revealing a momentary glimpse of something more raw, more genuine, before it was quickly smoothed over.

“Just answer the question,” said Marcus. He tapped his foot against the leg of the table impatiently.

"Well, if you must know, art has always been a passion," he said.

“I am something of a black sheep in my family. I come from a long line of investment bankers, but I decided to take the road less traveled. I studied art history at Yale.”

“How brave of you,” said Hayden dryly.

“It might not seem like it now, but it was very important to my family that I follow in their footsteps. But I always knew I wanted something different.”

Hayden took note of his response and looked on with focus.

"From the time I was a child, I have always had a gift for it. I had a gallery in New York for a while. We started out small, this little place in Brooklyn, and then, before you knew it, I had a place on the Upper West Side. I was the first person to sell a Yorick Van Ericson, you know."

Hayden nodded, pretending to know who that was and not to be too impressed by it.

She couldn’t help but feel a little out of her depths in front of this man. As arrogant and annoying as he was, he did have an expertise in the art world that she would never have access to, due to her previous job as a sketch artist before entering the FBI academy. The world of fine art was still a closed door to her, no matter how badly she wanted to be accepted into it.

“But you’re in Seattle now?”

“And where better to surround oneself with beauty than in a place like this?" he leaned back, as though he could glimpse the skyline through the concrete walls of the field office. “We get so much rain here; we need to bring some of the beauty of the world inside.”

Hayden nodded, pretending to consider his words while her mind raced. Was his love for art sincere, or just another layer of varnish applied to his façade? She needed him talking, not posturing, if she was going to uncover the truth behind his polished exterior.

"You see," he continued, his voice now a blend of nostalgia and pride, "I've always had a love for the craft. Art isn't just about aesthetics; it's an investment." He flashed a glance at Hayden, one corner of his mouth lifting in a half-smile.

"You mean you paint yourself?"

"Well, no, actually." He frowned briefly. Hayden knew that critics like him were a dime a dozen— people who were happy to criticize other people's art without ever lifting a brush to paper for themselves.

"But I have a good eye. And you can make a pretty penny."

"Is that so?" Hayden said, her tone light, but her eyes sharp, dissecting his every gesture. "Do you think we could have a look at your security cameras?" she asked.

"I would, but I'm afraid we erase them every 12 hours."

Hayden frowned, knowing that this was unlikely to be useful.

"Speaking of personal investments," she pivoted towards him abruptly, "didn't you invest time in yoga classes? I heard you had an interesting rapport with your instructor; Laura, was it?"

Miles stiffened, as if the name had triggered an imperceptible electric shock. He laughed, a little too forcefully, "Laura? The name doesn't ring any bells."

Hayden watched as he avoided her gaze, his fingers betraying him as they drummed lightly on the edge of the table. Marcus stepped forward, arms folded, an unspoken signal of solidarity.

"Odd," Hayden pressed, "because I've been told you were quite the regular. It seems unusual to forget someone you saw frequently." She wasn't actually sure if this was true. It was a bluff, but one intended to force him to make a mistake.

The drumming stopped, and Miles's face tightened. He exhaled slowly, a calculated release of tension.

"Ah, Laura," he conceded, as though the name had finally surfaced from the depths of his memory. "Oh, you're going to laugh when you hear this. You're going to wish you hadn't wasted your time."

"How so?"

"Yes, we did have a minor disagreement. Nothing noteworthy. She declined my invitation to dinner, and I may have overreacted."

"Overreacted?" Hayden echoed, allowing the word to hang in the air between them, laden with implication. As she exchanged a glance with Marcus, the shared suspicion was palpable. They both knew there was more to this casual admission than Miles was letting on.

Hayden leaned forward, her elbows resting on the table. The overhead bulb cast a halo around them but did nothing to soften the growing tension. "Miles," she began, her voice steady and probing, "where were you the night of Laura's murder?"

The question lingered, suspended in the air like the dust motes dancing in the light. Miles's eyes shifted, darting from Hayden to Marcus, then back again. His lips parted as if to speak, yet no words emerged. He seemed to grapple with an invisible adversary, his throat working silently.

Marcus's brow furrowed, a silent testament to the gravity of the moment. Hayden watched Miles closely, noting every flicker of emotion that crossed his features. There was a palpable hesitance, a refusal to answer that spoke volumes. She could feel the certainty settling in her bones; he knew more than he was letting on, and his passion for art wasn't the only thing hiding behind those sharp blue eyes. Anger, perhaps, at being spurned by Laura?

"Your silence is quite telling, Miles," Hayden pushed further, her tone hinting at the severity of the situation. "A jury wouldn't need much more to be convinced."

Hayden knew that this was probably a bluff, too, but it was a good one.

“I’m not so sure about that,” said Miles. “You know, I have the money to hire a good lawyer. And right now, all you have is that I didn’t get a date with a yoga teacher. Not exactly a smoking gun.”

“Even still, legal fees are very expensive these days,” said Hayden. “Who knows if you could sway a jury, but the court can never prove you innocent. It can only prove you not guilty. I wonder what your high-end clients would think about your involvement in a case like this.”

“Are you threatening me, Agent Smart?” he said, leaning over the table.

“Not at all,” she said. “I am simply explaining to you why it is in your best interest to tell us everything you know.”

That seemed to strike a chord. Miles straightened up, his hands finding refuge in his pockets. "Look, I..." he began, and there it was—the crack in his facade. "I wasn't anywhere near Laura that night. I had other... engagements."

"Engagements?" Marcus echoed, unimpressed.

"Deals," Miles corrected himself, the word sour on his tongue. "I was across town, tied up in a deal." His gaze finally met Hayden's, a flicker of defiance—or was it desperation? —flashing in his eyes. "Not the kind you'd want to brag about."

Hayden's heart quickened at the admission, realizing they were peeling back layers of deceit far beyond what they had imagined. A shady deal was not an alibi, yet it offered a glimpse into the man before them—a man who, while capable of duplicity, might just be innocent of murder.

Hayden leaned in, her gaze unyielding, "More," she demanded. "If you weren't killing Laura, what were you doing?"

Miles slouched against the chair, his eyes flickering to the side before he surrendered the truth. "I was selling a forged Monet to Mitchell Carson."

"Carson?" Marcus interjected incredulously, "The tech billionaire?"

"None other," Miles admitted with a rueful tilt of his head. "His mansion on Mercer Island. He fancies himself an aficionado." A bitter laugh escaped him. "Thought he could outsmart the system with his money."

"Forgery is a serious crime, Miles," Hayden warned, the edge of disappointment sharpening her voice as the lead they had chased dissolved into nothing more than another art world scandal. But it wasn't as serious as murder.

"I thought that's what this was about," Miles said, a weary resignation settling over his features. "You're not the first ones looking into my... extracurricular activities."

"Even so," Marcus chimed in, his stance rigid, "we'll have to report it."

“Hey, what happened to saving my reputation?” he said. “I helped you; you help me.”

“I'll see what I can do,” said Hayden. Even if she didn't like Miles as a person, she had to honor the spirit of their agreement.

As they turned to leave, Hayden took a final glance at Miles, his figure deflating into the shadows of the interrogation room. The weight of the unsolved case pressed upon her shoulders, the image of Laura's lifeless form haunting her thoughts. They had uncovered a fraud, but the true perpetrator remained a specter in the night.

CHAPTER TEN

Erica Stanton took another bite, fork idly tracing the remnants of tiramisu on her plate. Her friends were still laughing over shared stories and sipping their wine, but Erica's gaze kept flickering to the sleek black watch on her wrist. Sensing a lull in the conversation, she placed the fork down and flagged the nearest server with a practiced wave. "Could I get the bill, please?"

"Skipping out on us already?" Jenna's voice held a playful note, but her eyes were curious as they met Erica's.

"Got a hot date or something?" Martin teased, leaning back in his chair with a knowing smirk.

She had known that her friends would react like this. They met for dinner every week, and they always gave her the same trouble if she tried to improve her love life.

"Something like that," Erica replied, her lips curving into a mysterious smile. She felt her cheeks warm slightly under her friends' scrutiny. The anticipation of the evening's possibilities fluttered in her stomach as she pulled out her credit card.

"Come on, spill it," Jenna urged, her interest piqued. "You can't just leave us hanging."

"Okay, okay." Erica leaned in, her voice dropping conspiratorially, her cheeks going warm.

"I received a note in my office mailbox today. No name, just a time and place."

"Ooh, a secret admirer?" Martin raised an eyebrow, intrigued.

"Exactly," Erica said, nodding. "And I have a hunch it's from the cute copy guy down the hall. You know, Don? The one with those deep blue eyes and that shy smile?"

"Copy guy, huh? I didn't take you for the office romance type," Jenna remarked, a hint of surprise coloring her tone. "Don't you have a policy about that kind of thing?"

"Well, what the boss doesn't know won't kill him," she answered, garnering a series of "oohs" and "okays" from the table.

Erica shrugged, tucking a loose strand of hair behind her ear. "There's just something about him," she mused, wistful yet confident. "Tonight might just be the beginning of something."

"Or the end of your singlehood," Martin added with a wink.

"Hey," said Stacy, from the back corner, "how do you even know that copy guy is the one who sent you the note? It could be someone you don't know or like at all. Could be a total creep."

Erica frowned. Stacy was always the stick in the mud, out of everyone in the group.

"Good point," agreed Jenna. "Tell me that you're at least meeting in a well-lit, public place?"

"Well…"

"You should be careful," said Martin. "Remember that time you went on that date with the guy who wouldn't stop talking about septic systems?"

Erica tried to laugh. "Don't remind me."

"Trust me," said Jenna, "It could be like that again. Or a lot worse."

"Either way, I won't find out sitting here," she said, signing the receipt the server had discreetly placed on the table.

"Just promise us you'll be careful. You never know."

"Thanks for the concern, but I promise that I am fine."

Erica stood up, slinging her purse over her shoulder, feeling the weight of her friends' gazes on her as she prepared to venture into the unknown.

The air outside held the crisp promise of a Pacific Northwest evening as Erica stepped out of the warmth of the restaurant. A few stray laughs from her friends chased after her, the sound mingling with the rustle of leaves along the sidewalk.

"Be careful," Martin called out, a cautious edge to his chuckle. "You never know with these secret admirers."

Erica turned, flashing them a confident grin that seemed to push away any shadow of concern. "I'll be fine," she assured them, the silver flecks in her eyes catching the glow from the streetlamps. "It's just the copy guy, not a serial killer."

With a playful wave, she pivoted on her heel and moved with purpose, her boots clicking a steady rhythm against the pavement. The city's nocturnal symphony rose around her—distant cars, the murmur of nightlife, the occasional siren—a backdrop to her own unfolding drama.

The note's words circled in her mind as she approached the waterfront, its instructions as clear as the reflection of the moon on the water. In her jacket pocket, her fingers brushed against the folded piece of paper, its creases worn from multiple readings.

The lines of poetry were etched into her memory now, each word a delicate thread weaving an image of desire and mystery.

"Like Venus, you rise from the waves of the mundane," she recited softly to herself, savoring the verse, feeling the anticipation bubble within her. The comparison was flattering, and for a moment, she allowed herself to feel like a goddess adrift among mortals, pulled toward destiny by the gentle tug of romance.

She had spent so many years working towards a flourishing career, that she had sort of forgotten about her love life.

It was exciting to think that someone would be interested in her. And she knew that if it turned out to be some creepy stranger, she could always turn and walk away.

The shore came into view, the water lapping at the edges like a lover's whisper against the skin. She paused, allowing herself a moment to take in the serenity of the scene—the soft waves, the scent of brine mixed with earth, the hushed rustle of leaves in the gentle breeze. This was the spot where the note had summoned her.

Her breath formed tiny clouds in the cool air as she waited, alone yet filled with the company of possibility.

Erica's heels clicked softly against the weathered boards of the pier as she advanced towards the water's edge, her silhouette cutting a slender figure against the sprawling canvas of Seattle's night skyline. The Space Needle pierced the heavens, a beacon amid the twinkling constellation of city lights. She always found the sight grounding, a reminder that ambition and dreams were rooted right here, in the concrete and steel.

She wrapped her arms around herself, feeling the crisp embrace of the evening air. Her heart danced a nervous rhythm, fluttering with the kind of excitement that was reserved for the unknown. As she peered out over the dark waters, Erica couldn't help but let her thoughts drift to the man who might soon share this view with her—the one whose words had promised adoration from behind the anonymity of a handwritten note.

"Please don't be like the rest," she whispered into the breeze, a private hope cast out into the vastness of the Puget Sound.

She wasn't merely thinking of the timid men she'd left in her wake, men wilting under the intensity of her drive, her career. She wasn't even thinking about the guy who spent their entire first date talking about septic tanks. She had gone through a long line of mediocre men who either couldn't hold a conversation or talked far too much about unimportant things.

Maybe the poetry was a good sign. Maybe that meant that this new admirer was capable of thoughtfulness.

No, she yearned for someone who could stand beside her, unthreatened, unwavering—a true partner in the dance of life's trials and triumphs.

With a sigh, Erica glanced at the delicate face of her watch, its hands moving steadily forward. Time seemed to mock her, each passing second an insistent drumbeat counting down to...what? A beginning or another disappointment?

"8:07," she murmured, noting the time with a furrowed brow. The agreed moment had come and gone, the minutes slipping by like grains of sand through her fingers. Doubt crept into the corners of her mind, casting shadows upon the thrill that had propelled her here.

She usually wasn't impatient when it came to these things, but he was the one who had suggested the time.

"Office romances," she mused, a wry smile tugging at the corners of her mouth, "not quite the punctual affairs of storybooks."

Despite her jest, a thread of concern began to weave itself into the fabric of her anticipation, a silent question mark arching against the backdrop of the waiting city.

And still, she stood there, the Venus of the note, gazing out across the water, hoping the tide would bring in more than just the driftwood and sea foam—hoping it would carry in the start of something new.

Erica tugged her coat tighter around her as a breeze stirred the night air, sending ripples across the dark water before her. Her breath formed little clouds that disappeared as quickly as they emerged, ephemeral as the hope that had started to wane within her. The Seattle skyline, moments ago a sparkling backdrop to her anticipation, now took on an aloof quality—distant and indifferent.

A chill of realization crept up Erica's spine, and she shuffled through the sand, the granules working their way into her shoes.

The note—the poem that had likened her to Venus—it could have been left by anyone. Her mind raced through the day's events, the bustling corridors of the courthouse where she'd defended the indefensible, fought for the downtrodden. Faces blurred in her memory; countless individuals had passed by her office, any one of whom could have slipped the note into her mailbox while she was locked in battle with the scales of justice.

"Anyone," she whispered to herself, the word tasting like bitter uncertainty on her tongue.

As a public defender, she stood at the crossroads of a thousand lives, each intersecting with the law in ways mundane or profound. Erica prided herself on her focus, her ability to sift through stories, to find truth amid the chaos. But now, it dawned on her just how vulnerable that made her to unseen forces, to silent observers who watched from the peripheries of her life.

This could even be nothing more than a silly prank, done by one of her friends or a defendant that felt slighted, designed to embarrass her.

The thought unsettled her, rooting her feet in the damp earth as if the gravity of her realizations added weight to her being. Maybe this rendezvous was folly, a moment of whimsy unbecoming of someone with her rigor. "Time to go home, Erica," she chided herself, the resolve setting in with each syllable.

She turned away from the water, ready to chalk up the evening to a lapse in judgment when movement caught her eye—a silhouette etched against the dim light, standing far too close for comfort. Her heart lurched, adrenaline surging as she tried to process the sight: a dark figure, unmoving, watching.

"Can I help—" Her voice broke off into the night, her question unfinished as fear seized her vocal cords.

In that split second, every courtroom confrontation, every late-night work session blurred into insignificance. Instinct screamed at her to flee, to escape the unknown intent written in the stance of the stranger behind her. But before she could act on the primal urge to run, to scream, darkness engulfed her world.

A rough hand, a cloth clamped over her nose and mouth—smothering, suffocating. Erica's arms flailed, her fingers clawing at the air, seeking purchase on something, anything. Her lungs burned for air that wouldn't come, her mind crying out in silent terror.

Then, nothing but blackness, deep and complete, as consciousness slipped away from Erica Stanton on the lonely shore, swallowed by the night.

CHAPTER ELEVEN

The glow of the computer screen cast an eerie pallor on Hayden's face as her eyes darted across the endless rows of data, images, and notes that cluttered the desktop.

The cursor blinked incessantly, a silent metronome measuring the stagnation of their investigation. She rubbed her temples, wishing a breakthrough to materialize. But the truth was as glaring as the stark white of the text document opened before her: they were at an impasse.

"Anything?" Marcus's voice cut through the silence like a lifeline tossed into the void.

She shook her head without looking up, the muscles in her neck tensing with the admission of their failure.

She was disappointed that Miles had turned out to be innocent. For a brief moment, she was convinced that the case would be simple, but she was beginning to realize that it would only get more difficult.

"It's like we're chasing a ghost through a maze with no exit." Her voice betrayed the weariness she felt bone-deep, a frustration that gnawed at her resolve.

Marcus leaned back in his chair, the creak of the faux leather echoing the strain of their prolonged vigil. The clock on the wall ticked mockingly, underscoring the late hour.

"We're not going to find anything new tonight," he said, a hint of resignation lacing his words.

Hayden wanted to argue, to insist that they press on until the tendrils of dawn crept through the blinds, but the futility of it lodged in her throat.

"Just a few more hours," she said. "There must be something else that we're not seeing."

"We've been awake for too long," he said, stifling a yawn.

She knew he was right. They needed rest, distance, a chance to reset their weary minds.

With a sigh, she pushed away from the desk, her movements sluggish with defeat. As she stood, the image of her cat, Pissarro, curled up on the windowsill of her apartment flickered in her mind—a beacon of normalcy in the maelstrom. The thought of her soft bed, the quiet hum of the city at night filtering through the cracks in her urban sanctuary, tugged at her. Even just a few hours would help.

"Okay," she conceded, her voice softer now, stripped of its earlier edge. "A few hours of sleep might give us a new perspective."

Marcus nodded, a knowing look in his eyes as if he understood her internal battle all too well. They gathered their things in silence, the ritual of departure a familiar one after countless nights just like this.

As Hayden reached for her coat, the fabric felt heavy in her hands, laden with the weight of unsolved secrets. But she draped it over her shoulders with a resolve that belied her exhaustion. Sleep would be her temporary reprieve, a chance to escape the case that consumed her waking thoughts—for a little while, at least. And perhaps, in the quiet solitude of her apartment, with Pissarro purring contentedly at her side, she would find the clarity they so desperately needed.

She was halfway through the door of the office, the dimly lit corridor outside promising a brief respite from the case's relentless grip, when the shrill ring of her cell phone sliced through the silence.

Hayden's heart skipped a beat at the sound, the harbinger of news she knew wouldn't wait till morning.

“Who is it?” asked Marcus from right behind her.

“Not sure.”

"Agent Smart," she answered, her voice steady despite the sudden tightness in her chest.

"I’m with the local police. Another one on the shore," the voice on the other end was gruff, the words tinged with a weary urgency that mirrored her own. "It's bad, Hayden. Worse than the last."

The world seemed to tilt on its axis, and for a moment, she leaned against the door frame for support. The prospect of sleep, of escape, evaporated as swiftly as it had appeared. She cast a quick glance back into the office where Marcus was collecting his keys, the silent question in her eyes meeting his resigned nod. There would be no reprieve tonight.

"Text me the details. We're on our way," she said before ending the call, the finality of her tone leaving no room for argument.

They descended into the parking garage, their steps quickening as they navigated between the slumbering cars. The city pulsed around them, oblivious to the darkness that had just tightened its grip.

"Quick stop," Hayden muttered, more to herself than to Marcus as they climbed into the car. "We need coffee."

The fluorescent glow of an all-night café flickered like a beacon as they pulled up.

Inside, the smell of freshly brewed coffee cut through the tang of fatigue that clung to them. They stood side by side at the counter, the scalding cups a small comfort against the chill that had nothing to do with the night air.

"Thanks," Marcus said as he took his cup, his gaze fixed somewhere beyond the window, where the night waited to swallow them once more.

Hayden lingered in one of the booths for a moment, drinking in her coffee, hoping that it would give her enough energy to get through the rest of the night. She had been reluctant to rest just minutes before, but now it felt like all chances of restoring her energy had been taken from her.

She took a breath and gave a great yawn.

“You ready,” asked Marcus.

“Give me one more minute,” she said, and then she took another sip of the drink.

"Okay. Let's go," Hayden replied, her thoughts already racing ahead to the shore.

Back in the car, they drove in an uneasy silence, the caffeine doing little to ward off the dread that settled in Hayden's stomach. When the kaleidoscope of police lights came into view, painting the night in strokes of red and blue, she felt a jolt of adrenaline cut through the haze of exhaustion.

Yellow tape cordoned off the scene, flapping in the breeze like macabre streamers at a celebration no one wanted to attend. Officers moved about with purpose, their faces set in grim lines as they acknowledged Hayden and Marcus with curt nods.

Hayden's hand found the badge hanging from her neck, the familiar weight a reminder of the duty that called her to this grim tableau by the sea. They stepped over the threshold marked by the tape, entering the chaos of another crime scene, another puzzle that demanded to be solved.

They were here now, in the thick of it, the dead of night their unwanted companion. And as the water's edge came into sight, the relentless whisper of the tide against the shore a mocking serenade, Hayden braced herself for what awaited them in the unforgiving embrace of the shoreline.

Their footsteps slid into the sand underfoot and punctured the muted hush that had fallen over the scene. A local officer, his badge glinting under the harsh glare of the floodlights, approached Hayden and Marcus with a solemn expression.

"Agent," he began, offering a nod to both before focusing on Hayden, "we've ID'd her." He extended a hand, within it a clear evidence bag containing a small, leather purse. "Found this just up the beach."

Hayden accepted the bag, the plastic cold and slightly damp in her grip. She peered inside at the ID, the victim's smile a stark contrast to the grim reality of the night. Marcus leaned in, his sharp eyes catching the name and age faster than she could process them.

"Any witnesses?" Marcus asked, his voice low and steady.

"None who saw the crime go down. Just the guy with the metal detector," the officer replied, jerking his head toward the distant figure of a man wrapped in a blanket, seated in the back of an ambulance. "He's shaken up but gave us the call right away."

"Good work," Hayden said, handing the purse back. Her gaze wandered past the officer, drawn irresistibly to the place where the tide caressed the shore, its rhythm now a somber lullaby for the tragic scene that unfolded beneath the moonlight.

The water, dark and whispering, lapped gently at the edges of a figure laid out on the sand. As they drew closer, Hayden could see the careful arrangement of the body – arms resting by her sides, legs straight, as if she were merely sleeping. But it was the artful outline of a seashell encircling the woman's feet, each stone painstakingly placed, that arrested Hayden's attention. The killer had left his signature once more, a chilling reminder of their inability to catch him.

The victim's hair, long and dark, fanned across her shoulder, spilling onto the sand like ink from a broken quill. Hayden felt a surge of anger at the desecration, mixed with the familiar pull of determination.

"Photos, measurements, everything," she instructed, her voice cutting through the noise around them as investigators buzzed about, documenting the latest horror. "I want to know how long she's been here, what he did, and why he chose this spot."

Marcus already had his notebook out, pen poised as he surveyed the scene, ready to catch every detail Hayden dictated.

They worked in tandem, a machine of flesh and bone fueled by relentless drive, even as the sea's endless churn seemed to whisper of mysteries yet unsolved, of lives snatched away too soon.

Hayden's gaze swept over the chilling tableau before her, a frigid draft of recognition icing down her spine. Even though she worked in the dark, she did her best to capture every detail, including the way that shadow and darkness pooled around the victim.

The pattern clicked into place with a nearly audible snap.

"It's 'The Birth of Venus,'" she murmured to Marcus, who had edged closer to hear her thoughts.

All she had to do was imagine the victim standing upright.

Her eyes traced the curve of the stones around the victim's feet, mirroring the shell from which the goddess of love and beauty was said to have emerged. The sea's gentle caress seemed to animate the scene with a macabre semblance of life, distorting the masterpiece into something sinister.

With each new crime scene, the killer wove a deeper narrative through the defilement of classical art. Hayden's mind raced, dissecting the layers of perversion laid out before them. The act revealed not just a murderer but someone with an intimate, albeit twisted, appreciation for Renaissance art. It both repulsed and fascinated her, this glimpse into the abyss of a psyche that found kinship in beauty and brutality.

"Venus," Marcus echoed, his tone subdued. He understood the implication as well as she did. Their adversary was not merely playing a game; he was communicating through the language of the old masters, selecting his victims as a painter might choose his subjects.

But admiration for the intellectual challenge paled beside the raw fear gnawing at Hayden's insides. Somewhere out there, another soul was marked for the killer's grotesque gallery. The thought spurred her into action, even as it sent a shiver skittering across her skin. She needed to step into the shoes of both artist and muse to anticipate his next strike. Time was slipping through their fingers like the sands beneath their feet, and with each grain, the danger grew for some unsuspecting target locked in the sights of a murderer with a penchant for infamous beauty.

CHAPTER TWELVE

Hayden's fingers brushed the cool, rough texture of her leather-bound notebook before she flipped it open. The muted symphony of police radios and the rhythmic whisper of the ocean merged into a distant murmur as she poised her pencil over a fresh page.

Her eyes narrowed, tracing the haunting outline of the scene before her: the stark contrast of the pale body sprawled on the dark sand, the cruel angle of limp limbs, the almost peaceful repose of the victim's face under the harsh glare of the crime scene lights. Representatives of the coroner's office, forensics teams, and crime scene photographers scattered around, taking pictures and samples to investigate.

People like Miles could try to keep art an exclusive thing, belonging only to the elite, but for Hayden, it was the way that she saw the world, the way that she found killers and kept people safe.

With each deliberate stroke of her pencil, Hayden's gaze dissected the tableau, committing every shadow and shape to paper. She sketched the curve of an arm, the sweep of hair matted with sand and seaweed, the eerie stillness that death had draped over the young woman who had once been vibrant and alive. Details mattered, and Hayden knew the art of observation was as crucial to her investigation as any scientific analysis.

She reflected on "The Birth of Venus" by renaissance painter Botticelli. She wondered what the killer intended by pulling from another painting in another era. After all, the style was deeply different from both "Girl with a Pearl Earring," and "The Dream."

Could he be referencing the different time periods and places that the work came from? Or did he pull randomly from it all, in order to better confuse her?

Was there a reason that this painting depicted a myth, that of Venus emerging from the foam of the ocean? Or did it simply fit the scene he had already chosen?

She considered all the implications of these questions as she worked.

As her drawing took form, Hayden's mind wandered through the labyrinthine motives of their enigmatic killer. Each victim had been staged with disturbing precision, referencing classical artworks that spoke of beauty and tragedy in equal measure. She pondered the twisted psyche behind such acts. Did the perpetrator fancy themselves a modern-day Caravaggio, painting in blood and flesh instead of oils? Or perhaps they were a scorned artist, their aspirations crushed by the gilded gates of the art world's elite, now seeking a perverse form of recognition.

Hayden shivered, not from the chill of the encroaching night, but from the cold realization that they were hunting someone who found macabre splendor in the act of murder. With a final flourish, she closed her notebook, her drawings a silent testament to the horror before her, and to the urgent need to catch a killer lost in his own dark gallery of death. The sound of her partner's voice interrupted her thoughts.

"Can you tell me what you were doing out here?" Marcus's tone was steady, designed to comfort yet extract truth.

The man's silhouette, cast by the high beams of a patrol car, bobbed slightly as he nodded.

Once she looked closer, Hayden could tell that his gray, thinning hair was slicked back into a thin ponytail, and he wore camo overalls, and old, sandy-covered boots.

"Yeah, I'm a treasure hunter," he said, his voice revealing a hint of pride amid the tremor of shock. "Been walking on this beach for years. You'd be surprised at what people leave behind. And what washes up. It can be pretty lucrative."

Hayden added a few last shading strokes to her drawing, capturing the contrast of light and shadow that played over the contours of the crime scene. The notion of searching for discarded treasures seemed so at odds with the grim tableau before her. She wondered if the killer too sought recognition, a twisted form of discovery for their grotesque displays.

"Lucrative, huh?" Marcus prodded further, but Hayden's attention wavered as she considered the night's revelations. Somewhere in this macabre exhibition lay the crux of the killer's message—a gruesome gallery where life mimicked art, each victim an unwilling muse.

Her fingers smudged the graphite, blending it into the grainy texture of the paper just as the sea blended sand and water on the shore. Every detail she captured, every line and curve, brought her closer to understanding the mind behind the horror. As the conversation between Marcus and the treasure hunter faded once again into the background, Hayden realized that the true treasure they sought wasn't buried beneath the sands but hidden within the layers of a murderer's deadly masterpiece.

Marcus's silhouette melded with the inky backdrop of the night as he leaned in closer to the treasure hunter. The man's gaze remained fixed on the gentle ebb and flow of the tide, his eyes reflecting the sparse moonlight that danced across the water's surface.

“It is lucrative, actually,” said the treasure hunter. “But that isn’t why I do this. It’s about the thrill of the chase, isn’t it? Uncovering something that has never been found, finding all things forgotten and left behind.”

Hayden frowned. She wondered if this was how she sounded when she talked about her pastime of drawing, or maybe even how she sounded when she talked about her full-time work.

"Is this your usual time for beachcombing?" Marcus's voice cut through the rhythmic waves.

Hayden was wondering herself if it was standard to go looking for things at this time of night, or if the man had any good reason to be there.

"Yup," the man replied without shifting his attention. "Best time for it, really. No crowds to speak of, and if I turn up something nice, there’s no squabble over who it belongs to." He paused, a faint smile touching his lips as though reminiscing on a particularly good find. "Plus, the tides are low. Makes for easier pickings. Don’t know if I’ll be able to come out here for quite a while, though."

This was his first comment about finding the body.

"I didn't want to believe it at first," he said. "The sight will follow me through my dreams, no doubt."

Hayden, her hand poised above the page of her notebook, caught the nuance in the treasure hunter's tone—a blend of satisfaction and solitude. She sketched the outline of the solitary figure, imagining him walking the moonlit beach, the solitary hunter in his private domain.

Marcus nodded slowly, making mental notes that Hayden could almost see forming behind his thoughtful frown. He crouched down, level with the man, mirroring his contemplative posture. "We’re going to look for DNA evidence in the coming days,” he explained. “Did you touch the body when you found her?"

The question seemed to pull the man back from the sea, his focus returning to the grim reality before them.

Hayden knew that this was the right question to ask, but she focused on her drawing.

"At first," he began, his voice a notch lower, "I thought she might've just been knocked out or something. Maybe sleeping. Didn't look like she'd been in the water long—wasn't bloated or anything, and no obvious injuries."

Hayden's pencil hovered over her drawing, the image of the untouched body etching itself onto the paper even as the man's words painted a picture in her mind—one devoid of the violence usually associated with their grim discoveries. It was the paradoxical serenity of the scene that unnerved her, the calm that belied the storm of cruelty that had ended a life.

"I got down on the ground to try to revive her," he said. "I have a CPR certification. Several years ago, I had to get it when I worked as a rafting guide."

"Rafting guide?"

"Oh, sure. I've done all sorts of things in my day. Rafting guide. Scuba diving guide. Deep sea spelunking dive."

Hayden raised an eyebrow. Who else would you expect to find combing the beach for valuables in the middle of the night?

"Okay," said Marcus. "What happened after that?"

"Well, I soon realized that she wasn't there anymore. And I called it in. Like anyone would."

She pressed the charcoal harder against the page, darkening the shadows, defining the stillness. In her rendering, the ocean's whispers became secrets shared between the shore and the sky, secrets into which a life had silently dissolved.

"I see," Marcus made note of that. "One of the crime scene techs will have to take a sample of your DNA to ensure that the fingerprints on the body align with your story."

"No reason why it wouldn't," said the man. "I wish I could be of more help. I looked around but didn't see anyone running away. Why people do things like this to each other." He shook his head. "I'll never understand it."

The man's palms were callused, his fingers trembling slightly as he recounted the moment of desperate intervention. His eyes flickered with the recollection of failure. "I just can't help think that if I had left my house a little earlier like I had planned, if I might not have gotten here too late." The weight of his futile gesture seemed to bow his shoulders, a silent apology forming in the downturn of his mouth. "I'm sorry for messing up your crime scene, officers."

Marcus exchanged a glance with Hayden, who had just sketched the final line of her third angle. Her detailed drawings captured not only the stark reality of the macabre tableau but also the finer nuances of the beach's nocturnal peace that had been so rudely shattered. With each stroke of her pencil, Hayden had dissected the scene, her analytical mind working in tandem with her artistic eye to seek out the truth hidden within the tragedy.

"Hey, you did what you thought was right," Marcus assured the man with a firm nod, his voice carrying the weight of authority tempered by understanding. "It is likely that she was poisoned, and there is nothing that you could have done to save her."

He straightened up and made a subtle motion with his head towards Hayden, signaling it was time to wrap things up.

Hayden met his gaze, her eyes sharp with intelligence and a hint of empathy for the man before them. In silent agreement, they both concluded the treasure hunter's heart had been in the right place, his hands guided by the instinct to save rather than to harm. The pieces of the puzzle in Hayden's drawings told them as much, corroborating the narrative the beachcomber had presented.

"Thank you for your help," Marcus said as he stepped back. "Don't leave town for a few days, and make sure to call us if you remember any other details.

They had gleaned all they could from this witness, and their pursuit of justice for the victim beckoned them elsewhere. Together, they turned away, leaving footprints in the sand beside the fading echoes of the lapping waves, another chapter in their search for the sinister artist behind the murders.

CHAPTER THIRTEEN

The first tendrils of dawn stretched across the sky, tingeing the horizon with shades of amber and gold. Gulls cried distantly as the sun peeked over the edge of the world, its beams striking the water and turning it into a rippling canvas of light.

Hayden leaned against the hood of her car, her eyes gritty from the weight of sleeplessness that hung on her like a heavy coat. Every part of her ached for rest, for a moment's reprieve, but the crime scene before her kept her tethered to wakefulness. She had been up for nearly forty-eight hours, and the edges of her vision were beginning to blur.

She pushed off the car, stifling a yawn that threatened to crack her jaw. The rising sun painted the scene in a clarity that the harsh artificial lights of the night could not. It was then, with the dance of light on the undulating waves, that something caught her eye—a scrap of paper partially obscured by the dark rocks at the water's edge.

"I signed up for this," she reminded herself.

Now, it looked like she would have to spend another day working with little rest to sustain her.

Hayden approached the water's edge cautiously, each step measured, her mind already turning over the possibilities. Her fingers, encased in latex, reached out and gently dislodged the note from its hiding place. She unfolded it carefully, her pulse quickening as she scanned the handwritten lines.

"Meet me at 8:00, where the water kisses the land," it read, followed by a few lines about Venus.

She wondered about the implications of the killer leaving this behind. It was probably a tactic used to get the victim in the right place.

The script was elegant yet hurried. A chill ran down Hayden's spine. This was no casual invitation. It was a siren's call, a lure. And Erica, poor unsuspecting Erica, had heeded its beckon only to be met with malice.

She recognized this for what it was: a piece of the puzzle deliberately left behind, a clue that was meant to ensnare Erica in a fatal trap. Poison, a voice whispered in the back of her mind, poison drawn by deceit and shadows.

The sun continued its ascent, indifferent to the tragedy it illuminated, as Hayden stood there, the note in her hand a tangible echo of a predator's design.

It was interesting to say the least that the killer had used a note to lure Erica out to the beach after dark. As far as she knew, he hadn't done the same with the other victims.

Could it be that Erica was too intimidating to confront head-on? Then again, he didn't confront any of his victims. He poisoned them almost immediately.

She wondered if deep down, the killer was deeply afraid of his victims, or at least didn't see himself as capable of being able to kill them on his own. He relied on the element of surprise.

Perhaps he knew that a note was the best way to get Erica alone, and he slipped it under her office door, mailed it to her, or left it for her to find on her desk.

She would have to check the cameras at the public defender's office to be sure.

Hayden started to wonder if the killer studied his victims, stalked them for a long time before striking, learning their comings and goings, so he would know when they would be alone.

She searched the paper for the tell-tale signs of fingerprints, but she knew that she wouldn't be able to find anything.

Hayden slid the note into an evidence bag, the deed almost mechanical, her training a counterbalance to the creeping fatigue. She sealed it with a precise flick of her wrist and handed it to the technician, who nodded solemnly, understanding the gravity of the find.

"Agent Smart," a voice called out from behind her. She turned to see a local officer approaching, his face etched with concern. "My name is Vick. I'm with Seattle PD. Before we handed the case over to the feds, I was doing some research for the head detective, and I thought you could use it."

"Okay," she said.

She braced herself for getting blamed that the case had fallen to her jurisdiction. Most of the time, officers were kind and handed over all their information readily, excited to move on to easier cases. But at the same time, she was no stranger to the frequent turf wars that sprung up between the police and the FBI.

"Yes," she answered. "We've connected the case to the work of a serial killer."

“I know,” said Vick. “I think I can help. While the others examined the crime scene, they sent me back to do a little research. And I did some digging and got some early statements from her friends. We've got something that might interest you."

"Oh,” Hayden said. “Thank you for your help. Go ahead," she said, her eyes not leaving the officer's as he pulled out his notepad.

"A friend of the victim called in with information about the case. I guess a few details leaked, and the press got wind of it. Might be the last person to see her alive before the killer. I interviewed her, and she has an alibi, but she says Erica mentioned she was meeting someone named Donovan that night. Works at the courthouse, photocopy department."

“How did she find out?” Hayden asked. “Is the case on the news?”

“I think someone leaked the name, and it made it on the local coverage this morning,” came the officer’s answer. “No other details.”

Donovan. As much as she hated everything being on the news, at least she had a lead. The name felt like a weight in her mind, dense with potential implication.

“Did she give a last name?”

“No. I started looking into it, but I got reassigned to a string of larceny cases.”

"Did she say anything else about him?"

"Only that Erica seemed... excited? You know, because she fancied the guy. I guess she’s had this crush on him forever. They work together. I wish I had more details. The friend was pretty distraught. It might be nothing, but if I were you, I would want to know."

"Thanks. This is a real lead," she replied, her brain ticking over this new information. Excitement turned sour – a tale as old as time.

With the rising sun warming her back, Hayden stepped away from the water's edge and the hushed conversations of the crime scene personnel. She needed space to think, to strategize.

She found a quiet spot beneath a willow tree, its branches a natural canopy creating a veil from the world's prying eyes.

It didn’t take her long to find the last name by looking into records of those who worked in Erica’s office. The full name was Donovan Hughes.

She needed to know more before she made him an official suspect. If there wasn’t anything there, then she would only waste valuable time. The question was a whisper lost to the morning breeze, but it propelled her forward into a world of maybes and what-ifs. If the note was indeed from him, then Erica's infatuation had been nothing more than a puppeteer's string, pulling her towards a deadly final act.

Hayden's fingers danced across the screen, tracing the digital footprint of Donovan Hughes. The glare of her phone cut through the dawn's soft glow, revealing a stream of muscle and sweat – the curated life of a man dedicated to physical perfection. Each tap was met with more of the same: the clink of weights, the flex of biceps, the proud display of chalk-dusted hands.

She counted the likes on each picture. A surprisingly high number.

Her eyes flickered with impatience as she swiped past endless selfies in front of gym equipment, each accompanied by captions extolling the virtues of discipline and protein intake. "Come on, give me something," she muttered under her breath, nearing the end of her patience.

The photos blurred into a monotonous parade of fitness obsession, each one seemingly disconnected from the crime that had unfolded by the water's edge. Doubt crept into her mind like an unwelcome shadow.

But then, almost as if the universe itself responded to her silent plea for a break in the case, something caught her eye. It was subtle – a mere sliver of reality amid the vanity – but it was there, undeniable in its significance. A year and a half back in the timeline of posts, tucked away in the corner of a gym mirror selfie, was a familiar face.

"Gotcha," Hayden breathed out, a spark of adrenaline igniting within her weary frame.

It was Naomi Cruz, reflected in the mirror.

She zoomed in, her fingers pausing over the image. The reflection revealed more than Donovan's triumphant pose; it unwittingly captured another narrative, one that potentially wove Donovan into the fabric of Erica's last moments. The background held the key—a bystander in this visual chronicle—but to Hayden, a beacon in the night.

Hayden leaned in, her eyes narrowing on the figure standing behind Donovan's flexed biceps and gleaming ego. The screen of her phone seemed to become a window into the past, the gym's mirror a portal that brought a ghostly witness into the present.

In the picture, Naomi's gaze fixed on Donovan with an ease that spoke of familiarity, her lips curled into an affectionate smile reserved for more than casual acquaintances.

Linking Donovan to one victim was a good sign, but linking him to two?

If she did a little more digging, maybe she would find that he was involved with both women.

Hayden still didn't understand why he might want to kill them. But she did know that most murders are done by someone that the victim knows. She scrolled the rest of his profile, looking for more information.

The connection bridged the gap between Donovan's seemingly harmless vanity and the shadow that loomed over Erica's untimely end.

He could have gained Erica's trust and then lured her to the beach with the note.

Determined, Hayden pocketed her phone and strode across the dew-kissed grass to where Marcus was wrapping up interviews with local onlookers. His brow lifted in question as she approached, his own fatigue mirrored in the lines etched around his eyes.

"Marcus," she said, her voice carrying the weight of newfound purpose, "I think I've got something."

He straightened, attention sharpening. "What did you find?"

"Naomi Cruz," she replied. "I have a new suspect."

"Great," he said. "I'm all ears."

"His name is Donovan, and he worked with Erica. That's who she thought wrote the note. And he spends a lot of time working out. In one of Donovan's gym selfies, Naomi is looking at him like he's the only guy in the room."

"Significant?"

"Could be. It's a lead, at least." Hayden watched as understanding dawned on Marcus's face. "And I have a hunch finding Donovan won't be a wild goose chase. He lives for the gym—a creature of habit."

"Consistency can be a weakness," Marcus mused, nodding. "Let's hope it's his."

"Exactly," Hayden confirmed. "If he's not there pumping iron, someone will know when to expect him. We'll get him to talk."

"Let's move then," Marcus said, a new vigor in his step. "The sooner we get answers, the better."

Together, they left the crime scene, the morning sun climbing higher in the sky, its light chasing away the shadows of doubt that had plagued Hayden moments before. Now, with every step towards the gym, she felt the edges of the puzzle coming together, each stride taking her closer to the heart of the mystery.

CHAPTER FOURTEEN

The automatic doors swished open, ushering Hayden and Marcus into the pulsating heart of exertion and sweat that was PrimeFit Gym. The clanks and grunts of heavy machinery and even heavier ambitions resonated through the air, setting a rhythm to the determined scuffles of sneakers against rubber matting. This was the sanctuary of the dedicated: where bodybuilders sculpted sinewy masterpieces, where cross-fitters forged their endurance like steel in fire.

In spite of the physical fitness exams that she had passed to complete her FBI training, she couldn't help but feel a little intimidated, watching those around her lifting weights that she didn't think possible for a human.

Hayden's eyes, sharp and assessing, swept over the forest of weight racks and the jungle of resistance machines, taking in the landscape of human endeavor. Her partner Marcus, with a build less Herculean, more a nimble boxer's, moved in sync beside her, his own gaze alert. They were an odd duo amid the sea of bulging muscles and barbells, but they had a different kind of strength.

"Can I help you?" The voice, dripping with condescension, cut through the clamor. A woman perched behind the front desk, her posture as stiff as the starched collar of her uniform, eyed them with visible disdain. Her fingers, lacquered in a hue of crimson arrogance, tapped impatiently on the glossy surface of the reception counter.

Hayden knew that she had been zeroed in on as someone who didn't fit. And she wasn't sure how a room fool of gym rats would accept hearing that one of their friends was under investigation.

"We're looking for someone," Hayden said, her tone professional yet carrying an edge that hinted she wasn't there for a casual chat about gym memberships. She bolstered herself by taking a deep breath. "Is Donovan here today?"

The receptionist's painted lips curled into a semblance of a smile, one that didn't reach her calculating eyes. "No, he's not," she lied smoothly, barely glancing up from her manicured nails.

Hayden raised an eyebrow.

Her keen sense of observation had already noted the man in question, unmistakable in his intensity, hoisting dumbbells in the far corner of the gym. He wore a ripped t-shirt. His focus was absolute, the weights rising and falling in a steady cadence that mirrored the unwavering lie of the woman before them.

"Is that so?" Hayden replied coolly, her gaze flicking momentarily toward the corner where Donovan's broad back rippled with each controlled movement.

She shared a look with Marcus, a silent exchange that conveyed their mutual understanding of the situation. The game was on, and they were all too familiar with how to play. If the receptionist wasn't going to help her, she would just have to let herself in.

With a determined stride, Hayden bypassed the front desk's glossy facade of hospitality. Her eyes were locked on Donovan, who was still engrossed in his routine, the plates clanking rhythmically as he completed another bicep curl. She navigated through the maze of weight machines and benches, her partner Marcus trailing just a step behind.

"Excuse me, Donovan," Hayden called out, asserting herself into his line of sight.

He barely acknowledged her presence, his gaze transfixed on the mirrored wall before him, muscles contracting with each lift.

The weights touched down with a rubberized thud on the padded floor, yet he did not turn to face her.

"You look a little lost. This isn't the ballet studio." His voice was somehow deeper than she thought it would be.

"Could have fooled me," she returned, unable to resist.

He growled.

Out of the corner of her eye, she could see Marcus getting more and more uneasy.

"We have a few questions to ask you," Hayden said. "Do you think you could put the weights down and talk to us for a moment?"

"I don't talk to cops," he said.

Hayden frowned, starting to get frustrated with his belligerent attitude.

"Well, maybe you want to avoid an obstruction charge."

"I work in the PD office. So, if you want to try, I have about ten people I can call."

"Great. Why don't you just step over here, and this will all be over very quickly."

"I'd love to help, but I'm a little busy. Or can't you see I'm in the middle of my set, detective?" His voice rumbled, dismissive, without a hint of curiosity as to why an agent might be seeking him out.

He looked over his shoulder at the receptionist who had failed to stop them. She gave him a disinterested shrug back.

He looked back in the mirror. He was clearly very impressed with his own physique and didn't think he had time to speak to Hayden.

"Listen, it's about an important investigation," Hayden insisted, undeterred by his standoffish demeanor. Her hands found her hips, her stance exuding both impatience and authority.

Donovan didn't respond immediately, allowing himself the time to finish his final rep with a grunt of effort.

Setting the weights back onto their rack with deliberate precision, he finally stood upright. Yet instead of facing Hayden, he strode purposefully towards the squat rack, slapping chalk dust from his hands in a cloud of indifference.

"Hey!" she protested, her voice cutting sharper this time. "I'm talking to you. I know you're busy, but this is a little more important than whether or not you finish your workout."

She drew the attention of the gym, bodybuilders turning her way. Suddenly, Hayden felt very small.

But Donovan seemed to move within a bubble of his own making, where the only thing that mattered was the iron in his grasp and the strain against his frame.

Hayden's jaw tightened, observing the blatant snub. She exchanged a brief glance with Marcus, her frustration mirrored in his clenched jaw. They were used to resistance, but this outright disregard was a new level of challenge—one Hayden was more than ready to meet.

Marcus, his patience threadbare, stepped into Donovan's path, a human barricade against the behemoth's singular focus. "That's enough, Donovan," he said, voice low but brooking no argument. He flashed his badge.

A feeling of a relief washed over Hayden. If Marcus used his rank as an agent to de-escalate the situation, she was all for it. But Donovan didn't seem to care.

For a moment, the gym's cacophony of clanking metal and grunts receded, as if the very air anticipated the collision of wills. Then Donovan's hand shot out, shoving Marcus with a force that sent him staggering back.

Hayden tried to step in between the two of them, but she got pushed into the squat rack and she had to fight to keep her balance.

"Workout's not done," Donovan growled, his eyes locked onto the squat rack as though it were a shrine to his personal creed.

"I think it is," said Marcus.

"What are you going to do about it, little guy? Your badges don't mean nothing here. These guys, we could take every last one of you."

He loomed over Hayden, and for a moment, he had a crazed look in his eye. She was worried that he would attack. She knew she should draw her gun, but her mind went blank, and in a room full of innocent people, she didn't want to risk anyone else getting hurt.

She prepared herself to get hit, when out of the corner of her eye, she saw Marcus getting off the ground.

"Damn it, Donovan!" Marcus recovered and lunged forward, pushing back hard against the mountain of muscle. His shove was met with a snarl, and suddenly the two men were a tangle of flailing limbs and fury, a storm of testosterone and aggression about to erupt.

Hayden's instincts kicked in.

Whatever sense had abandoned her in the previous moment returned. She couldn't let this escalate—not here, not now. Slipping through the fray with agility honed from years on the force, she wedged herself between them just as a punch from Donovan whistled through the air where Marcus's head had been a heartbeat before.

"Enough!" Hayden commanded her voice a sharp crack.

She caught Donovan's wrist, using his momentum to spin him away from Marcus. As Donovan stumbled, disoriented, she applied a deft hold she'd practiced a thousand times in training—using leverage, not strength, to bring the larger man down.

Donovan's bulk hit the gym floor with a thud that stilled every other movement in the vicinity. He lay there, surprised and winded, while Hayden stood over him, her breath coming fast but even.

"Time to talk, Donovan," she said, her tone leaving no room for further workout delays or resistance. Marcus, rubbing at a shoulder, nodded his silent approval. "You are under arrest for hindering a federal investigation."

They were a team, and Hayden had just proved that muscle was no match for method.

The silence in the gym was absolute, a tangible void where the clank of weights and grunts of exertion had once filled the air. A collective gaze turned toward Hayden as she stood with an assertive posture over Donovan's prone form. Her chest heaved lightly from the adrenaline, yet her face was the picture of controlled professionalism.

"Up," she commanded crisply, her voice slicing through the hush. Donovan, his expression a mix of confusion and indignation, pushed himself up to a sitting position. Hayden didn't wait for him to stand; she reached down, grasped his arm firmly, and assisted him to his feet.

"Let's be clear," Hayden said, her eyes scanning the faces of the astonished onlookers who were still processing the sight of the takedown. "You're not being asked, Donovan. You're being told." With a flick of her wrist, she sent her hair cascading over her shoulder, a subtle but unmistakable signal that she was in control and unshaken.

She couldn't help but feel a little bit proud. She'd managed to take down a bodybuilder in the middle of his own gym. She quickly got out her cuffs to prevent him from trying to run away. She noticed a few respectful nods as she made her way towards the door.

Marcus, having recovered his bearings, stepped forward to join her. The two detectives formed an undeniable barrier between Donovan and any further thoughts of resistance. As they began escorting him through the maze of weight racks and benches, Donovan regained some of his bravado.

"I don't know what this is about. I promise. I didn't do anything!" he protested with a growl, shrugging against their grip. His voice carried a note of desperation, perhaps the first crack in his confident exterior.

"Save it for the station," Hayden replied, undeterred by his protests. Her grip tightened just enough to remind him that struggling wasn't in his best interests. She could feel the eyes of the gym patrons following them, the silent respect hanging heavy in the air.

Together, they emerged into the daylight, the cool outside air contrasting sharply with the heated atmosphere they left behind. They maneuvered Donovan into the backseat of their unmarked vehicle with practiced efficiency, ensuring he was secure before slipping into the front seats themselves.

As Marcus started the car, Hayden met Donovan's eye in the rearview mirror. His scowl was met with her unwavering gaze, a silent testament to the gravity of the situation awaiting him. Today, the gym's drama had been just a prelude to the real workout he'd face under the hot lights of an interrogation room.

CHAPTER FIFTEEN

For the second time in two days, Hayden stood opposite the interrogation room door, looking through the one-way glass, arms folded.

"That was pretty impressive back there," said Marcus.

"I'm just glad no one got hurt," Hayden said. In the moment, the surge of adrenaline in taking down Donovan had felt good, but once the feeling faded, she wasn't sure it was the safest way to keep things going.

"Still," he said, "someone had to put that guy in his place. He's pretty belligerent. How do you think we'll get him to talk?"

Hayden took a deep breath. She had been asking herself this very question for the past hour.

"I don't know," she admitted.

"I say we try to scare him. Tell him about the charges. Maybe tell him we have witnesses talking about an argument between him and Erica?"

Hayden shook her head. "I think that's the wrong move. The harder we push, the more stubborn he'll be. I think we just ask him our questions about the case, and if more evidence comes forward, we follow it."

Marcus nodded thoughtfully. "The tactful approach?"

"You saw how he reacted when we pushed him. I think he'll just feel cornered and become more reactive, not helpful at all."

"Okay," agreed Marcus. "I trust you."

The door to the interrogation room swung open with a force that left no doubt about Hayden's mood. Even though she didn't want to push him, she knew that she couldn't act like a doormat either. She wanted to demand his respect without coming off as threatening.

Her jaw was set, her eyes ablaze, and her gait purposeful as she strode into the starkly lit chamber, each step resonating against the cold, hard floor. Donovan sat on the other side of the table, his demeanor cocky as ever, but there was a flicker—an almost imperceptible shadow—that crossed his face upon seeing the fury in Hayden's approach.

Without a word, Hayden pulled out the metal chair next to Marcus and settled herself down with a clatter that echoed off the walls. She could feel Marcus's tension beside her, the slight wince he tried to mask as he shifted in his seat, no doubt the remnants of the earlier scuffle leaving him tender. Yet, she noted the set of his mouth, a line of determination that told her he was committed to seeing this through, bruises be damned.

"Let's get to the point," Hayden said, her voice cool and steady, belying the storm of anger within. She fixed Donovan with a stare designed to unnerve, to dismantle the bravado he wore like armor. Today, she would be the one to stand up, to show Donovan that his reign of intimidation had come to an end.

“We’re here to discuss a very important case that we’re investigating regarding one of your coworkers.”

“Well,” he said, “Whatever it was, it couldn’t have been me. I have no idea what you’re talking about.”

Hayden turned her head. He certainly acted belligerent and defensive for someone who hadn’t done anything wrong.

Donovan's fingers drummed an anxious rhythm on the steel table, a stark contrast to Hayden's stillness. She leaned in slightly, her gaze unwavering and sharp as broken glass. "Why come at us like that in the gym, Donovan?"

He looked down at the table. “The gym is my place, okay? I get a little touchy when people try to come in between me and my place.”

Hayden raised an eyebrow. “Even when an arrest is on the table?”

He didn’t answer.

Hayden leaned forward over the table. “Believe it or not, Donovan, I want to help, okay? That’s what I’m here for. All I want is to find the truth. But I can’t do that if you don’t talk to me.”

His bravado crumbled, replaced by something that resembled humility. He stopped his nervous tapping and met her eyes. "Look, I'm sorry, okay?" His voice, usually booming with self-assuredness, wavered. "I've been going through some stuff... a bad breakup. It's no excuse, but my emotions are all over the place. Anger management issues. That's what one of those shrinks said. Suggested I go to the gym to blow off steam. And recently, it has really helped. I've even made a few friends with some of the other regulars. And I've noticed a little more attention from the ladies at work." He winked.

Hayden didn't know how to respond. He had lashed out at the gym, but like she thought, when he didn't feel quite so cornered anymore, he let his guard down.

He sighed, a deep, ragged sound. "I didn't mean to lash out. If I hurt you or your friend, I apologize."

Hayden's brow lifted, surprise flickering across her features. The apology sounded genuine, which was not what she had expected from someone who thrived on intimidation. But sincerity wasn't evidence, and her gut told her there was more to this than just heartache.

"Right," she said slowly, processing his words while keeping her suspicion close to the chest. "Now, tell me about Erica. How well do you know her—the lawyer from your office? Was she one of the women giving you more attention at work?"

Donovan blinked, confusion momentarily overtaking his expression before he regained his composure.

"Erica? Yeah, I know her. She's—it's a big office, but she's alright. She's one of the PDs. Damn good one from what I hear around the water cooler too." He shrugged, the casual gesture belying the tension that had crept into his shoulders.

"Had she been giving you any special treatment?"

"Maybe. I guess. I don't know. She'd stop by the copy room sometimes, make a point to ask me about my weekend. Always laughed at my jokes. That kind of thing. Nothing out of the ordinary."

"Did you two ever get into any fights? Any kind of disagreements?" asked Marcus.

He lowered his brow, as if offended by the question.

"No, of course not. Why? What's this about Erica? Did she do something?"

"Not exactly," said Marcus.

Donovan's gaze drifted to the ceiling, his forehead creasing as if he were sifting through a catalog of faces in his mind. After a pause, recognition sparked in his eyes.

"Of course not. What was I thinking? Erica is a cool girl," he said, nodding to himself more than to Hayden. He leaned back in his chair, arms crossing over his chest defensively.

"Was cool," Hayden corrected gently but firmly, watching for any flicker of reaction. "She was found dead last night."

The muscles in Donovan's jaw twitched, and his arms fell to his sides. He looked genuinely taken aback, his usual swagger nowhere to be seen. "Dead?" he echoed, disbelief shading his voice. "That's... man, that's messed up. She didn't deserve that."

There was a note of sorrow there that seemed real, a far cry from the bullish persona he projected in the gym. If he was pretending to be surprised, then he was putting on a convincing performance.

Hayden let the moment of silence stretch, then shifted gears. "What about Naomi Cruz? Tell me how you two know each other."

"We hit the weights together sometimes," Donovan replied, his gaze shifting to the table, avoiding Hayden's piercing stare. "She's tough, can lift more than some of the guys. I respect that." He paused, scratching the back of his neck, an awkwardness settling over him. "I asked her out once. Just once. When she said no, I backed off. No hard feelings. Then I got involved with that other girl. The one who just broke up with me, and that's when I started to have problems with my anger."

"No hard feelings at all?" Hayden pressed, noting the way his eyes flickered before meeting hers again.

"None," he insisted, but something in his tone suggested a bruised ego, a hint of pride that had been dented but not quite broken. Hayden filed away this observation, alongside the sincerity of his earlier remorse and the surprise at the grim news about Erica.

"No," he said, throwing his hands up.

Hayden leaned forward, the metal chair scraping against the sterile floor of the interrogation room. Her eyes remained locked on Donovan's, searching for any flicker of deceit. "Where were you last night, around eight o'clock?" she asked, her voice steady despite the frustration simmering beneath the surface.

"Does it matter?" he asked.

"Both women were found dead earlier," Hayden explained. "We'd like to know where you were at the time of death."

Donovan shifted in his seat, his fingers drumming a nervous beat on the table.

"Dead?" he asked, looking surprised. "Are you sure?"

Hayden raised an eyebrow.

"But I just… I don't…She didn't deserve that. Neither of them did."

He gave a deep sigh." Look, since Amanda and I split, things have been rough," he started, a vein throbbing in his neck as he spoke. "I've been crashing at the gym a lot. I haven't found a new place to live yet. I've got to get my name off the old lease first, but she can't cover the rent by herself, so it's a whole mess.

Hayden felt sorry for him, not being able to fully leave his girlfriend after things had gone bad.

“They've got this small room for personal trainers to catch some rest between sessions." He swallowed hard, his gaze flickering to the one-way mirror before returning to Hayden. “They’ve been really kind to let me stay there. But if my work found out, they’d probably fire me, professionalism, and all that. That’s where I was last night.”

“Can anyone confirm that?” she asked.

"There's security footage covering the front and back doors. It'll show I was there all night."

"Security footage," Hayden echoed, her mind racing with the implications of his alibi. She tapped her pen against her notepad, the sound echoing in the silence that followed.

Donovan nodded, relief washing over his features. "Yeah. It's time-stamped and everything. I can't be in two places at once, right?"

"Right," Hayden conceded, though each word tasted like ash in her mouth. With a deliberate motion, she stood up, signaling the end of their conversation. "We'll verify the footage. If your story checks out, you're free to go for now."

As Donovan rose from his chair, there was a noticeable slump to his shoulders, a stark contrast to the bravado he'd worn like armor in the gym.

But before he left, he looked back at the two detectives. “I’m sorry I wasn’t more help. Do you think that Naomi and Erica were killed by the same person?”

“Looks that way,” answered Hayden.

He shook his head. “I can’t believe it. That I knew both of them, and they both… That someone would do something like that. I know I have my problems with anger, but…” he trailed off. “I guess I should go. Sorry again about what happened at the gym.”

“It’s no problem,” said Hayden.

“And thanks for believing me.”

Hayden watched him exit, the door closing with a soft click behind him.

Left alone in the suffocating quiet of the room, Hayden's hand curled into a fist. Another dead end. She exhaled slowly, willing her heartbeat to settle. The case was cold, and every lead seemed to slip through her fingers like sand. Frustration gnawed at her, but she pushed it down, letting it fuel her resolve instead. Somewhere, amid the tangled web of lies and half-truths, lay the thread that would unravel this mystery. And she would find it, no matter how many dead ends she faced.

With the growing pressure from the media and bodies piling up, she'd have to work harder to bring the killer to justice.

CHAPTER SIXTEEN

The engine of the old van ticked as it cooled, a low murmur against the suburban soundscape. Parked beneath the dappled shade of an overhanging oak, its faded logo and peeling paint were a testament to countless journeys now concluded. Within this quiet alcove of the apartment complex, the vehicle was unremarkable, nondescript—a chameleon among the domestic and the mundane.

A light rain fell; in this city it was almost constant. The man in the car scowled. He used to love the sunlight, but now he only wished that the rain would fall heavy enough to make a sound on the roof of his car, and not this halfway business, that wasn't really a storm nor a nice day.

He sat motionless in the driver's seat, his eyes fixed on the second-story window across the courtyard. The blinds were tilted open just enough to create slats of visibility, granting him fragmented glimpses of the life within. A hint of movement, a shadow passing by—the subtleties of existence that most would overlook, but he noticed them all. He had always been attuned to such details; they were the essence of his craft, the silent language of forms and figures that he once translated onto canvas with brushstrokes bold and delicate.

Now, though, his observations served a darker purpose.

His gaze sharpened as she appeared behind the blinds. Even through the imperfect view, her face was unmistakable features etched into his memory with the precision of a master sculptor.

The curve of her cheek, the prominence of her brow, the way her hair tumbled in a cascade of rebellious curls, the shape of her nose; these were nuances he had studied with the intensity of a man possessed.

She was unaware of the eyes that followed her every move, oblivious to the danger lurking just beyond the confines of her sanctuary. In fact, she didn't think to look out the window at all. To her, the world outside her window was just a backdrop for her daily rituals, a tableau upon which the sun cast its ever-changing light. But then again, people never did pay much attention to their surroundings. That was why they needed artists, to pay attention for them. To distill the world and all its beauty into something that demanded their attention.

The woman in the window turned out to be no different, too focused on the reflection in her mirror to notice the world outside her window.

He didn't care.

For his purposes, it was better that way.

She thought that she was about to go about yet another ordinary day, paying attention to nothing.

But to him, she was the centerpiece of a grim composition, a subject that compelled and enraged in equal measure. She represented an audience that never applauded his talent, a world that refused to see him as he saw himself—an artist deserving of recognition and reverence. And in this moment of silent surveillance, he savored the irony of his invisibility, for it granted him the power to watch, to wait, to plan.

A slight parting of the blinds, and their eyes almost met—a fleeting connection severed by layers of glass and anonymity. He didn't flinch or turn away. Instead, he leaned back into the seat's worn upholstery, a predator patient and calculating, biding his time until the moment was ripe.

Tessa Rodriguez leaned closer to the window, her fingers working deftly as she traced the outline of her eyes with a pencil. The natural light filtering through the half-open blinds was kinder than the harsh glare of bathroom bulbs, forgiving the minute imperfections that only she seemed to notice. Her features came alive with each stroke of makeup: a subtle contouring here, a dab of color there; by the time she finished, her face was a canvas ready for the night's impending spectacle.

He found himself wondering what kind of brush she was using, what the shade of her foundation was.

She stepped back, surveying her work with a critical eye. Not many would choose the afternoon's waning glow to prepare for a shift, but Tessa found something soothing about the routine—it was a ritual of transformation that marked the boundary between her private life and the persona she adopted behind the bar.

Her apartment, though modest, bore the evidence of a life rich with experiences. Photos with friends, captured mid-laugh or mid-dance, adorned the walls. A bookshelf overflowed with well-thumbed novels and volumes on mixology, her dual passions living side by side. But it was the collection of odd trinkets—a napkin with a lipstick-stained kiss, a coaster scrawled with a stranger's phone number—that hinted at her knack for drawing stories out of even the most reticent of patrons.

Tessa was more than just a bartender; she was the confidante of night owls and lost souls. With a practiced ear and an empathetic nod, she could spin their tales into sagas, making each customer feel like the protagonist of their own epic.

She doled out advice with the same care she applied to crafting cocktails, knowing when to offer a consoling word and when to share a hard truth. The man watching wasn't sure where she got all this information from or where she'd gained the wisdom. As far as he could see, she hadn't lived much of her own life, and she spent her days directing the decisions of other people, who half the time were too drunk to remember.

She glanced at the clock. It was almost time. Slipping into her shoes, she gave herself one last look in the mirror. The woman staring back was ready to step onto the stage of the dimly lit bar, where every night promised new encounters and fresh anecdotes. With a final adjustment of her blouse, Tessa grabbed her keys and headed out the door, leaving behind the quiet comfort of her sanctuary for the lively hum of her workplace.

He sat there, hands resting on the steering wheel, eyes fixed on the second-floor window of Tessa Rodriguez's apartment. From this unassuming vantage point, he had watched her countless times, studying her routine with an artist's keen observation.

Through the slats of the blinds that veiled her life from the outside world, he'd seen the flicker of her silhouette, moving with the grace of someone who knew their body was just another tool to ply their trade.

She was a great bartender. Even if he was suspicious about her so-called life advice that she doled out for free, he knew that she was good at mixing drinks.

Tessa's artistry wasn't splashed onto canvas or etched into marble—it was poured into glasses and mixed under dim lights, garnished with a slice of human connection.

He had gone inside one day to investigate for himself.

He had to get every detail just right. He had to know every detail of her day.

He had been just another shadow at the bar, nursing beers she poured without seeing him.

He was surprised how easy it was to avoid her notice amid the rush of customers, all vying for her attention.

It was part of his research, to understand his subject from the mundane angle of an everyday patron. While she regaled others with anecdotes, her gaze never lingered on him, never noting his presence—he was like a ghost, unseen yet fixated on every gesture she made, every word she spoke.

In those moments, he found himself acknowledging her talent.

Just as he manipulated colors and shapes, she manipulated spirits and emotions, blending them into concoctions that loosened tongues and softened barriers.

Those regulars at the bar trusted her, for some strange reason. Maybe not because of what she said, but because of how she said it. She had a talent for making people like her.

She was a sculptor of social fabric, teasing out threads of people's lives and weaving them into stories worth retelling. To the regulars who leaned against the polished wood of the bar, seeking solace in the amber glow of whiskey and the warmth of her smile, Tessa was more than a bartender; she was the maestro of their evening escapades.

He wondered if it was not, at the end of the day, manipulative. Just a way to get bigger tips. A way to trick people into thinking that you had a relationship with them.

From behind the grimy windshield, he watched as the light in her apartment blinked out. Like him, she prepared for the performance of a lifetime each day, not on sprawling gallery walls, but within the intimate stage set by four corners of a bar. And though they were artists of vastly different mediums, they shared the relentless pursuit of perfection in their crafts. She, with her shakers and bottles, he, with strokes and lines—both masters in their own right, yet unnoticed by the other in the intricate dance of predator and prey.

The van's steering wheel felt cold and unyielding beneath his clenched fingers, a stark contrast to the heated rush of blood that surged through him with each pounding heartbeat. Fury bubbled up from the pit of his stomach, an acidic swell that threatened to erode the composed facade he had so meticulously built. He deserved recognition—his art should have demanded it—but the world was blind, willfully ignorant of the genius that lurked in the shadows.

He released the wheel, flexed his fingers, and let out a slow breath aimed at quelling the tempest inside. His eyes, however, remained locked on the apartment above, unblinking and intense. They followed

Tessa as she moved with graceful efficiency within her domain, a silhouette framed by the soft light spilling through her window blinds.

Then, with the suddenness of a scene change, she appeared outside, key in hand, the door clicking shut behind her. She descended the steps, oblivious to the spectator in the van, whose gaze dissected every aspect of her being. As she slid into her car, the engine came to life with a purr that carried to him on the breeze, a reminder of the distance between observer and observed.

In that moment, as if viewing his reflection in the rearview mirror of her departure, he realized the transient nature of their crafts. Her fame, earned night after night, pouring drinks and spinning tales, would evaporate like the last traces of alcohol on an abandoned glass. And his? Even more ephemeral—a shadow cast briefly upon the wall before being swallowed by darkness.

Both artists were destined to be overwhelmed by the next rising star, the new flavor of the month. It was a cruel truth, but one that brought a twisted sense of camaraderie to his solitary vigil. As Tessa's car merged with the flow of traffic, disappearing from view, the anger within him subsided, replaced by a cold resolve.

No matter how fleeting their marks upon the world, he would ensure his lasted just a little longer, seared into memory by the fire of his actions to come.

CHAPTER SEVENTEEN

The fluorescent lights overhead seemed to flicker in rhythm with Hayden's throbbing temples. Each report, each crime scene photo blurred into a smeared canvas of red and black as she fought the fatigue clenching her mind.

Her fingers, stiff from hours of typing, hovered over the keyboard before she let them fall with a sigh. The lives of the victims whispered secrets just beyond her grasp, and she knew that somewhere in the minutiae lay the breadcrumb trail to their killer.

"Research," she murmured to herself, eyes flitting across the open files on her cluttered desk. It was there; it had to be. With a weary hand, she reached for the latest victim's dossier, the edges worn from frequent handling.

She reviewed all the security footage she could find, played on two screens, looking for something to stand out.

Nothing did. All the cars that passed by any of the crime scenes vanished just as quickly. There were almost no people on foot, and they were all clearly seen walking away from the crime scenes, not further into the blind spots where the crimes took place. This killer had been careful to cover his tracks.

Just then, the click of the door announced Marcus's return. His shadow fell across the papers strewn about, his figure a stark contrast to the chaos of the investigation. He set down a steaming cup of coffee beside her—a peace offering from the world outside their bubble of case files and unanswered questions.

"Okay, so that lead with Donovan did not go where I thought it would," he said.

"I know," said Hayden. "Who knew bodybuilders could be so sensitive?"

"I wouldn't go that far," Marcus smirked. "I'm not sure sensitive is the right word for it, but when you backed off, he relaxed and told us what we needed to know."

Hayden nodded. "I just wish it had turned out to be more useful. We still have a killer on the loose, and we're no closer to finding him."

"Maybe we're looking at this all wrong," Marcus said, pulling up a chair with a scrape that jarred Hayden's fraying nerves.

"We've ruled out finding a suspect with DNA or fingerprint evidence. We could also start questioning people who've bought arsenic in bulk. There's got to be a lead there."

Hayden looked up at him, her eyes reflecting the countless dead ends they'd already encountered. Her mind raced through the implications of his suggestion, weighing it against the heavy curtain of exhaustion that veiled her thoughts. But deep down, the insistent drumbeat of intuition told her that the answer was closer than they thought, tangled in the personal histories they had yet to fully unravel.

Hayden's fingers drummed a staccato rhythm on the wooden surface of her desk, each tap a silent rebuttal to Marcus's proposal. She lifted her gaze to meet his, the hollows beneath her eyes darkened by sleepless nights.

She shook her head. "That will never work. I think we should take a different route."

"Won't work? It could lead us right to the killer."

"Bulk purchases? That's too simple, too traceable." Her voice was steady, but her mind buzzed with the chaotic dance of facts and hunches. "Our guy is smarter than that. He could've used a fake ID, or maybe swiped the arsenic from some unsuspecting gardener or chemist. And he might not have bought it in bulk."

Marcus leaned back in his chair, arms crossed, his skepticism etched into the furrows of his brow. "So, what? You want to keep wading through the victims' pasts? We've been down that road, and so far, it's turned up empty because—"

"Because it matters," Hayden interjected, more sharply than she intended. She reached for a photo of one victim, tracing the edge as though it would yield more secrets. "We need to understand them—their connections, their routines. Why them? I know it hasn't gotten us anywhere yet, but I think if we keep digging, then it could."

The words tumbled out, a plea to the universe for clarity.

He shook his head, dismissing the idea with a wave of his hand. "It's speculative. And everyone is way more connected than we think. We're bound to find a coincidental commonality between all of them at some point. We need concrete evidence, not wild guesses based on who they shared a coffee with five years ago."

"Speculative?" Hayden pushed back her chair, the screech of its legs against the floor mirroring the tension between them.

"Since when did you start believing that investigation is speculative?"

"I don't mean it like that. I'm just saying that this could give some concrete leads."

"So could my plan. Why can't you see that? These were people, Marcus. With lives that somehow intersected with a killer's twisted game. There's a pattern here. I know it."

Marcus ran a hand through his hair, the weariness in his eyes mirroring her own. "And if this wastes our time? If we chase shadows instead? It's because these were real people that we have to take the course of action that will yield the fastest results."

"There's just as likely a chance of finding the wrong suspect with your methods. If we look into the families and personal lives, then at least we're chasing something real," she said, her conviction burning bright against the fatigue that threatened to consume her. She turned back to the files, her resolve as unwavering as the question that haunted them: Why were these victims chosen?

The silence stretched between them, heavy with unspoken thoughts, until Hayden began to sift through the reports once more, searching for the elusive thread that would lead them to the heart of the darkness they hunted.

The tension in the room had become almost palpable, a thick fog of frustration that settled over both detectives. Hayden's hands were balled into fists, her knuckles whitening with the grip.

"This is about being thorough, about not dismissing a possible lead because it doesn't fit into your neat, little box of 'concrete evidence.'"

Marcus leaned against the doorframe, his arms folded across his chest, a barrier to her accusations. "Hayden, you're so tunnel-visioned right now, you can't see the forest for the trees. We have to consider every angle, even the ones that don't align with your theories."

"I'm open-minded!" She shook her head, disbelief etching deep lines across her forehead.

Their gaze locked, two opposing forces caught in a standstill, each waiting for the other to yield.

"You call discarding my approach open-minded? Being attached to one theory isn't how we solve cases," he replied, his voice steady but edged with exasperation. "You know this. We need to be adaptive, look at all the variables. It's investigative work 101, Hayden."

He was using that condescending attitude that she couldn't stand. How did it always seem to come to this?

But as the seconds ticked by, the energy seemed to seep from Hayden's stance, her shoulders slumping ever so slightly as the weight of their shared exhaustion bore down on her.

She was beginning to question if they were effective partners when the real reason for their long argument dawned on her.

"God, I'm tired, Marcus," she admitted, her voice losing its earlier fervor. "We both are. And it's making us... it's making me stubborn."

Marcus's posture softened, the defensive set of his shoulders eased. "I'm sorry too, Hayden. We're just chasing our tails at this point, running on fumes."

He stepped closer, his tone gentler now. "Let's just... take a breath, okay?"

She nodded, the fight draining away as quickly as it had flared up. "Yeah. A breath sounds good."

"I do trust you," he said. "I just want to do this right."

"I do too," she answered.

"Good."

They stood there for a moment, two agents too weary to hold onto anger, the silence between them now filled with an unspoken understanding. The case was taking its toll, but they were still a team, united against the darkness that lurked in the files spread out before them.

"This case," she said. "The killer has beaten me at every turn."

"We'll find him eventually," said Marcus. "I just hate seeing more people get hurt in the meantime."

"I know," Hayden said. She had trouble giving up the blame when people died in the middle of cases. She thought again of Erica, and wondered if she could have saved her.

But she knew she couldn't go there. She was too tired, and it would only distract her from her work.

With a deep breath to clear her head, Hayden reached for the stack of reports, their edges frayed from constant handling.

She knew that if she looked long enough, then she could find something that would help them in the case.

"You know," began Marcus. "We haven't slept in a while. I say we both go home for a little sleep, and then get back to its first thing in the morning."

Hayden almost didn't hear him. She was still reading the case reports.

The junior detectives had been thorough, compiling every scrap of information they could find on the victims' lives. She scanned the pages, eyes alert for any detail that seemed out of place, any connection they might have missed in their fatigue-fogged state.

“Hayden? Did you hear me?”

As her gaze skimmed over an interview transcript, a line caught her attention and she paused, rereading it slowly. A friend of Erica's had mentioned, almost in passing, that Erica had taken up art classes at a local community center. Hayden leaned back in her chair, a piece of the puzzle clicking into place. It wasn't much, but it was something new, a fresh lead that they hadn't explored.

"Marcus," she called out softly, not wanting to break the fragile truce that had settled between them. "I can’t believe I missed this detail from the statements taken by the local police.”

“What detail?” he said with a yawn.

“Erica was taking art classes," she said, pointing to the line in the transcript. "At the community center downtown.”

“Umm…” he looked from left to right. “I mean, how could we have missed that?”

“You’re right. It could be nothing, but because the killer has an art background, it’s probably something."

"It's something we didn't know before," Marcus finished for her, a spark of interest lighting his tired eyes. "Naomi did something similar. She enrolled in a weekend workshop there last fall." He straightened up, his mind visibly working through the implications. "Hayden, if the killer is staging the bodies like famous works of art..."

"Then maybe he met these women at some kind of art class." Hayden nodded, feeling the weariness lift slightly as the gears in her brain started turning again. "Extensive knowledge, even. This community center could be where our killer learned what they needed."

"I think that rest will have to wait a little longer,” Marcus said, pulling his laptop closer. "I'll look into the class rosters, see if there are any overlaps or recurring names."

"Good idea." Hayden felt a flicker of their old partnership rekindling. They were a team again, no longer at odds but united by a shared determination to unravel the mystery before them. As Marcus delved into the digital records, Hayden turned back to the reports, her focus renewed. This case had consumed them both, but now, with this new thread to follow, there was hope that they might finally bring the killer into the light.

CHAPTER EIGHTEEN

After a few more hours of research, Hayden found something interesting.

"Marcus, look at this," she said. "Looks like two of our victims took classes at the local community art center."

He leaned over her shoulder to look at the record. "With the same teacher too. One Sylvia Warren."

She did a quick search for the woman's name, and found that until recently she had taught ceramics at the local university. "Let's get going, then."

Hayden meandered through the vibrant corridor of the community center, her gaze drifting across a kaleidoscope of creativity that adorned the walls. She smiled as she looked at the wonderful images around her.

Here, a cluster of cheerful finger paintings, blobs and streaks of primary colors merging into abstract interpretations of childhood joy. There, the intricate detail of a photorealistic charcoal sketch by one of the teachers captured the delicate interplay of light and shadow with such precision that it nearly leapt from the canvas.

She paused before the sketch, studying the deftly rendered contours of a weathered face, each wrinkle telling its own silent story. The scent of dried paint and clay lingered in the air, a poignant reminder of untamed creativity that seemed to breathe life into the stillness of the hallway. It was easy to forget the weight of her badge, the coldness of her gun holstered discretely beneath her jacket as she lost herself in the artistry before her.

A soft sigh escaped Hayden's lips. This was where her heart truly lay—in the quietude of an artist's sanctuary, amid the rustling of brushes and the soft scratching of pencils against paper.

Longing tugged at her, an old friend beckoning her to set aside the files and photographs of her current case and instead surrender to the lure of blank canvases waiting to be transformed.

For a fleeting moment, Hayden imagined herself settled into one of those classrooms just beyond the hall, a palette of colors spread before her. She could almost feel the bristles of a brush between her fingers, the cool, sleek texture of wet paint gliding over the surface, each stroke a small act of creation. Her detective's mind, so accustomed to dissecting scenes and searching for hidden truths, yearned instead to explore the nuances of shading and the impact of paper texture on the vibrancy of a painting.

"Focus," she whispered to herself, a gentle chiding. Duty called, pulling her back from the precipice of her daydreams.

She knew that her skills were best used elsewhere. She turned her attention to looking for security cameras, something that would help with the investigation. Of course, there were none.

She had long since dedicated any artistic talent she had to observing the visual details of crime scenes, memorizing the faces of unknown subjects.

With a final, lingering look at the charcoal portrait, she pressed onward, feeling the familiar hardness of her determination settling back into place. Art may have been her first love, but for now, justice required her unwavering attention.

Marcus caught Hayden's gaze lingering on a vivid oil painting that depicted a stormy seascape, the brushstrokes wild and untamed like the waves it portrayed. He cleared his throat to announce his presence beside her.

"Thinking of a career change?" he teased lightly, his eyes crinkling at the corners in a friendly challenge.

Hayden offered him a half-smile, turning from the painting with a wistful glint in her eye. "Sometimes," she admitted, her voice softening with the confession. "I dream of opening my own studio one day—after my time at the Bureau is done."

"Art and crime-fighting," Marcus mused, nodding thoughtfully. "Maybe you could paint all those crime scenes that really stick in the imagination."

“Yeah,” she said. “Like there’s a market for that.”

She frequently wondered what her art would have focused on if her sister had not disappeared, throwing her down a very different life path.

"Art was my first love," Hayden said, her tone suggesting a reverence for a path not taken. "But it was never in the cards.”

“I knew you liked drawing, but somehow this is still surprising.”

“What, you never had a hobby?”

“Sure,” he said. “When I was a kid, I thought I was going to be a baseball player.”

“Really? Why do you never talk about it?”

He shrugged. “I don’t want to bore you.”

“Well, you underestimate me. I think that I could… learn to listen to you talk about baseball.”

“If I can listen to you talk about art, then I suppose anything is possible,” he joked.

“But let's find Sylvia Warren. We need answers, and I have a feeling she could help us unearth a few."

Their initial investigation into the art center had shown that the two victims had taken classes with the same woman, who also happened to be recently laid off from her job working at a university. Hayden wondered if some kind of conflict had gone down between the women, and with the added stress of a job loss, Sylvia had lashed out with violence.

Women made up such a small percentage of all murderers, but Hayden wouldn’t let that distract her from a good lead.

It made sense, given that the killer didn’t use physical force to overpower the victims.

Together, they navigated through the labyrinth of corridors, the sounds of pottery wheels spinning, people mixing paints, adjusting easels, all behind closed doors. The door to the pottery classroom stood ajar; they stepped inside to find Sylvia, her sleeves rolled up, hands submerged in soapy water as she scrubbed at the clay-caked wheels.

The room was filled with shelves lined with clay pots and cups in all stages of the process, some with glassy smooth exteriors and others that were clearly waiting to be thrown into the furnace.

"Ms. Warren?" Hayden called out, drawing the woman's attention.

Sylvia looked up, pushing a strand of damp hair away from her face with the back of her wrist. "Can I help you?" she asked, drying her hands on a towel.

"We were hoping to talk about your job here at the community center," Marcus said, his gaze taking in the rows of shelves lined with various stages of ceramic work.

She frowned. Hayden wasn’t sure that she would want to talk about jobs of any kind after the blow that she’d had to her university career.

“Well…”

Hayden showed her badge before she could refuse. “We’re with the FBI,” she explained. “We’re hoping you could help us answer some questions about a case.”

"Of course," Sylvia replied, gesturing for them to come closer. "It's been a blessing, really, being able to continue teaching after... well, it's a long story." She gave them a tight-lipped smile, the weariness in her expression hinting at battles fought and lost.

"Looks like you've made quite an impact," Hayden observed, noting the meticulous care with which the pottery had been crafted. It spoke of a teacher who invested more than just time into her work—an artist dedicated to her craft and to those she instructed.

"Teaching is my passion," Sylvia said, warmth returning to her voice as she glanced around the room that held much of her current life's work. "And these wheels," she added with a fond pat on the nearest one, "they keep me grounded."

Hayden nodded, understanding the solace one could find in their artistry. Whether it was the pursuit of justice or the creation of something beautiful from nothing, there was a kind of peace there—a refuge from the storms outside.

Hayden shifted her posture slightly, the detective in her rising to the fore as she noticed a shadow crossing Sylvia's face. "You mentioned it's a long story," Hayden prodded gently, resting her hand on the cool surface of a pottery wheel. "The job here being a blessing, after what happened at the university?"

Sylvia's hands stilled, and she glanced down at the dark clay residue that stained her fingers. "Yes, I was let go from the local university," she said, her voice tinged with bitterness that seemed to leach from her very soul. "They called it 'restructuring,' but we all knew it was just another word for budget cuts."

"Must have been quite the blow," Marcus chimed in, his tone one of sympathetic curiosity.

"More than you can imagine," Sylvia replied, her eyes hardening as they met Hayden's. "Years of my life dedicated to that institution, only to be dismissed without so much as a thank you."

Hayden caught the edge in Sylvia's words, the disdain for the place that had unceremoniously discarded her like yesterday's newsprint. An ember of suspicion glowed within her; anger could be a powerful motivator, and the wounds of pride ran deep. Yet before she could fan that ember into the flame of interrogation, Sylvia continued, her expression shifting to one of reluctant acceptance.

"Still, I understand the realities of academia. The arts are always the first to suffer when the purse strings tighten." She shrugged, a sense of resignation wrapping around her words like a shroud. "I've seen it happen before. It's never easy to accept, but what can you do?"

Hayden observed Sylvia closely, searching for any telltale sign that might indicate her feelings were more than mere frustration. But the woman before her stood composed, the anger seemingly ebbed away as quickly as it came, replaced by the weariness of someone who had fought this particular battle too many times.

“We’re investigating a case related to someone I think you knew. Erica Stanton and Naomi Cruz. Both of them took your classes.”

Sylvia's hand moved instinctively toward a shelf of misshapen clay pots, her fingers tracing the curves and edges with an artist's intimacy. "Erica was a standout," she confessed, her voice softening at the memory. "Her touch with the clay was like watching someone with a sixth sense for the medium. Naomi seemed to think that she was a better model than artist."

Her eyes glazed over, lost in a sea of what-ifs as she pulled down a ceramic piece that held a swirl of colors vibrant enough to capture a sunset.

"But Erica was truly talented," Sylvia continued, placing the pot back with reverence. "You don't see that often. There used to be a time when a gift like that meant something. But these days? Talent doesn't pay the bills, not in this industry." A wistful sigh escaped her lips as she wiped her hands on her apron, stained with the evidence of her passion. "If it did, I'd be as rich as those CEOs and founders. The art world—it doesn't care about potential unless it comes with a price tag. Erica knew that, too."

Hayden nodded solemnly noting her use of past tense, her detective's mind filing away each emotional current that rippled across Sylvia's face. She needed facts, timelines, alibis. "Sylvia, where were you the last two nights?" Hayden asked, her gaze steady and expectant.

“Why do you ask? You don’t think I’m involved?”

“Answer the question,” said Marcus.

“I’d rather not speak about my whereabouts. You get it. Privacy and all that.”

“Why did you say that she ‘had’ talent,” Hayden asked.

“What do you mean?”

“Are you aware that both women were found dead recently?”

“No. I didn’t know anything about that. I only said ‘had’ because as far as I knew, neither one of them are in the arts anymore.”

“Alright,” said Hayden. “So help me clear something up. Where were you the last two nights?”

“I would rather not say.”

“We understand,” said Hayden. “And we don’t want to make you divulge something that you’re not comfortable with. But this is important, and if we can’t get a clear sense of where you were, then you might become more of a suspect.”

Sylvia ran a soapy hand through her hair. “Fine.”

She stood and began to stack the clean pottery wheels around her.

"If you must know, I was driving," Sylvia answered promptly, reaching into the pocket of her apron. She produced her smartphone, tapping the screen a few times before swiveling it around to show Hayden. "Started ridesharing to make ends meet after the university cut me loose. Here, look—every fare I've taken is tracked."

Hayden leaned in, scrutinizing the digital map dotted with lines crisscrossing through the city streets. Each route timestamped, none veering close to the sandy outskirts where waves met land. No beach, no clandestine meetings under the cover of darkness. Just the sporadic zigzags of a person trying to stitch together a living.

"Looks like you've been busy," Hayden remarked, handing back the phone. Inside, her suspicion waned, logic painting a clearer picture than her initial gut reaction had. But she reminded herself, cases weren't closed on alibis alone. There was still much work to be done.

CHAPTER NINETEEN

Hayden got back into her car to leave the community art center. Even if she wanted to question Sylvia further, she couldn't argue with GPS data.

"Marcus," Hayden said, her voice low, "we're on the wrong track."

The lines on Marcus's forehead deepened slightly as he got back into the car next to her. He knew that tone, the one that said Hayden had hit a wall and was about to tear it down brick by brick.

"I guess she wouldn't be able to fake an alibi like that," he said, though the question was just for formality's sake. He trusted her instincts more than anything.

"Positive." She tucked the notepad under her arm, already mentally sifting through the facts and discarding the irrelevant. "Let's get back to the field office."

They pulled out of the parking lot in silence, the air thick with unspoken agreement. Back at their home base, Hayden slipped into her zone, the world narrowing down to the wide expanse of desk littered with crime scene photos and her collection of charcoal pencils. She pulled out a fresh sheet of paper, the white expanse staring up at her, demanding answers she hadn't yet found.

As she sketched out possible connections and timelines, Marcus paced behind her, his mind buzzing with questions and theories. He knew better than to interrupt her when she was in this state — it was like trying to stop a freight train mid-track.

Marcus watched from a corner, leaning against the cold metal of a filing cabinet, his arms folded across his chest. There was an almost meditative quality to Hayden's methodical sketching, each stroke of charcoal bringing the gruesome scenes to life. Her brows pinched together in concentration; she retraced lines and shadows, searching for the elusive detail that had remained just beyond her grasp.

"Anything?" Marcus finally broke the silence, knowing better than to interrupt unless necessary.

Hayden didn't look up, her hand moving steadily. "Not yet," she said, "but I will find it. I have to."

“So, does this really work?” he asked.

“Hasn’t failed me yet,” she answered.

They continued, two special agents, bound by the silent oath to seek justice, even if it meant revisiting the darkness time and time again.

Hayden's fingers smudged the charcoal across the paper, her strokes deliberate as she sketched the outline of a woman's delicate jawline. The scene in front of her was starting to take shape, the room falling away until all that remained was the artwork and the imagined victim within it. She focused on capturing the serene expression that had graced the face of the "Girl with a Pearl Earring" in Vermeer's masterpiece, attempting to see the room from the killer's twisted point of view.

“That’s two bodies found close together,” she said. “This killer is moving really fast. Escalating.”

Marcus nodded. “Usually indicates a good deal of anger. I think that given the escalating pace, he’s building towards something. We just don’t know what.”

“I wonder why he chose these paintings,” she wondered aloud. “Do you think that he saw something in the victims that reminded him of them?”

“Or maybe he just likes the paintings?” wondered Marcus. “Art is a mystery to me.”

“Well, it means something. We just have to figure out what it is.”

Hayden was unsure what to think.

The victims weren't just bodies; they were stand-ins for art, carefully arranged to mirror the timeless beauty found in oils and canvas. Hayden leaned back, her gaze flicking between the crime scene photos and her own recreations. Did the killer feel powerful, an artist in their own right? Or was there a deeper longing, a desperate need to preserve something they felt the world had overlooked?

"Odd way to get inside a killer's head," Marcus's voice cut through her concentration.

Startled, Hayden looked up to find him standing over her shoulder, his dark eyes scanning her work. There was a hint of bemusement in his tone, but he held back any judgment.

"Sometimes you have to step into their shoes... see what they see," Hayden replied, defending her unorthodox method without breaking her intense focus on the drawing.

Marcus nodded, his expression turning somber. He picked up his ringing phone.

Hayden's blood ran cold as she listened to a cryptic series of "yes" and "maybe" and "thank you," as he listened to whatever was being said on the other line.

She feared the result, and waited impatiently, until he finally confirmed her worst suspicion.

"Well, you might want to put on another pair. Another body was found."

A cold pit formed in Hayden's stomach, her hand pausing mid-stroke. The news hit her like a physical blow, the weight of failure pressing down.

Each victim was a life she had hoped to save, and now there was yet another to account for. If she had been able to find out what the connection to art really meant before now, she might have been more help.

"Where?" she asked, her voice barely above a whisper, the charcoal pencil rolling from her fingers and staining the desk with its mark. She was afraid to speak any louder than that.

"Abandoned warehouse on the east side. We should go—now."

She nodded, pushing back from the table, her mind already racing with the grim possibilities of what awaited them. The sketches lay forgotten on the desk, a silent testament to the urgency of their quest for justice.

The two detectives made it out of the building and quickly got into the car, ready to examine the next crime scene.

The tires of their unmarked vehicle screeched as they came to an abrupt halt outside the dilapidated structure that loomed ominously against the fading light of dusk. Hayden's breath quickened as she and Marcus dashed towards the entrance, their footsteps echoing through the vast emptiness of the abandoned warehouse. Yellow tape fluttered in the breeze like grim pennants, marking the threshold of another macabre tableau.

Inside, the air was thick with the metallic scent of blood and the musty odor of neglect. Shadows clung to the corners where weak streams of light fought a losing battle against the encroaching darkness. Police officers moved around with purpose, their somber faces etched with the all-too-familiar weariness that came with scenes like this.

"Agent Smart?" A uniformed officer approached, nodding towards the center of the space where a small congregation of forensics personnel were gathered. "Thanks for getting here so quickly. I've been placed in charge by Seattle PD until you guys arrived."

“What do we have?” she said, not wanting to waste time on formalities.

"The victim’s name is Tessa Rodriguez," the officer explained.

Her heart sank at the mention of the name, a silent prayer for the lost soul slipping through her thoughts. Tessa Rodriguez—a life reduced to a name on a report, a new piece in an ever-expanding puzzle that seemed to have no edges.

"She's a bartender. Apparently, a pretty popular one too, by the information that we've gathered."

"Any idea how long she's been here?" Hayden queried, her voice steady despite the turmoil inside. She needed facts, anchors in the chaotic stream of information that threatened to sweep her away.

"Can't say for sure," the officer replied, shrugging helplessly. "The body was found by the building inspector. Guy was doing a routine check before the owner lists it back on the market."

"Routine," Hayden murmured, irony not lost on her. Nothing about this was routine. The killer had struck again, leaving behind a gruesome signature that mocked their efforts to catch him.

But he must have known that the building would be empty. He was careful, covering his tracks at every turn, planning the most pristine crimes so that nothing went wrong.

"Thanks," she said with a nod, stepping past the officer to take in the scene herself. Her eyes scanned the area, seeking out those elusive details that might reveal what everyone else had missed. Every clue, every strand of evidence could lead them closer to the monster hiding behind these atrocities. But first, she had to understand the story laid out before her—the narrative woven by a killer who turned death into a perverse form of art.

Hayden's boots crunched on the detritus-strewn concrete as she approached the body, her breath forming misty clouds in the cold air of the abandoned warehouse.

The dense air smelled like mildew, and the windows were foggy and dirty. There was garbage littered across the ground from vagrants that had clearly been staying there just a few days before.

Tessa Rodriguez sat propped against the wall, an eerie stillness to her pose that was at odds with the brutal end she had met. The victim’s head was tilted elegantly over her left shoulder, eyes closed as if in peaceful slumber rather than the sleep of death.

Hayden searched her memory for a painting that she recognized, but couldn’t think of one that resembled this.

A string of pearls lay cool and lustrous against her throat, catching the weak light that filtered through the broken windows above.

In Tessa's lifeless arms, a dead ferret was cradled with a kind of mock tenderness, its small body limp and incongruous in the human embrace. Hayden noticed a black string tied tightly around Tessa's forehead, stark against her pallid skin. It was a tableau morbidly staged, each element a calculated placement.

This was a strange turn, and she didn't know what to make of it. Clearly, the killer's staging had escalated to the next level, making things more gruesome and darker.

For a moment, Hayden's mind refused to make the connection; this couldn't be another of the killer's pieces.

The scene felt disjointed from the pattern, a random act of violence perhaps.

But as her gaze lingered, the realization crept up on her with the inevitability of a shadow stretching across the floor at sunset.

"Alright, Michelangelo," said Marcus behind her, "what painting is this supposed to be?"

She searched her mind, knowing that it was familiar, and then the answer hit her, clear as day.

"Damn it," she whispered, the words barely escaping her lips. But Marcus's reference to a Renaissance painter triggered a memory.

"It's 'Lady with an Ermine' by Leonardo da Vinci," she said, a cold feeling settling over her skin.

"Didn't that guy invent things?"

"Yeah, he also painted. You know," she looked over at him in disbelief, "the 'Mona Lisa?'" Could he really be so unfamiliar with any art that he didn't know the most famous painting in the world?

"Oh, yeah," he said, the recognition dawning on him.

"This one is another classic painting. Here it is grotesquely mimicked."

Hayden's hands balled into fists at her sides, nails digging crescents into her palms as a wave of grief washed over her.

She should have seen this coming, should have pieced together the clues faster, anticipated the killer's next move. If only she had, maybe Tessa would still be breathing, still be a part of the world beyond this dreary canvas of death. A heavy burden settled on Hayden's shoulders, a weight made of could-haves and should-haves that no amount of resolve could lift.

"Another masterpiece," she murmured, irony bitter on her tongue. The killer had not only claimed another life but had done so with the same deranged artistry that haunted her waking hours. Hayden knew then that this chase was far from over, and the cost of justice was proving far too steep.

CHAPTER TWENTY

The next morning, after finding Tessa's body, Hayden was the first one in the office.

The first shards of daylight crept through the blinds, casting a geometric pattern across the spartan office floor as Hayden arrived. She cherished these solitary hours before the cacophony of ringing phones and clacking keyboards filled the space. Her fingers danced over the filing cabinet's cold metal handle, withdrawing the stack of dusty folders labeled with years gone by.

She and Marcus had both gone home for some much needed rest after initially examining the crime scene where Tessa's body had been found. There wasn't much they could do for the time being, and now with a clear head, the whole affair seemed a little less hopeless.

She settled at her desk, the chair creaking under her weight—a familiar symphony to her morning routine. The files fanned out before her like a deck of cards, each one a potential missing piece in the puzzle that had consumed her for weeks. With methodical precision, she leafed through them, pausing only to sip her lukewarm coffee.

As she delved deeper into the archives, Hayden's brow furrowed. There were plenty of mentions of Erica, notes scribbled in the margins, reports of sightings and whispers of her life outside of work. But Tessa? It was as though she existed in the shadows, her presence barely registered on these yellowed pages.

"Morning, Hayden," Marcus greeted as he entered, his arrival signaled by the faint jingle of keys. His eyes were sharp, carrying the weight of sleepless nights spent chasing leads that often led nowhere.

He seemed a little chipper, but maybe that was just the coffee in his hand.

"Marcus," Hayden acknowledged him without lifting her gaze from the papers. "You're here early."

"Couldn't sleep. Did a little research when I woke up first thing." He shrugged off his jacket, draping it over the back of a chair. "Listen, I was thinking—maybe we should visit Tessa's workplace. Talk to the people who knew her best."

Hayden considered the suggestion, her hands still on top of the paperwork. She had been so overwhelmed by the investigation, but this seemed like as good a starting place as any.

Marcus had a knack for seeing angles she sometimes missed, an instinct honed from years of navigating the labyrinthine streets of their city and its secrets.

"Good idea," she replied, finally looking up to meet his gaze. "We need to understand her, get a feel for her life beyond what these files aren't telling us."

"Exactly," Marcus said, nodding. "And if there were any messages, anything out of the ordinary, her coworkers might have noticed."

"Let's do it." Hayden closed the folder in front of her, determination steeling her features. There were answers out there, hidden in the fabric of Tessa's everyday interactions, and they were going to unravel them, thread by thread.

"I'll drive," she offered.

She stood up from her desk and made her way down the stairs to the car, Marcus close behind.

The two didn't talk much in the car ride towards Tessa's bar. There wasn't much need to. Both were deep in thought about the case, wondering how much longer it could go unsolved.

Marcus pushed open the heavy, varnished door of the "Onyx and Heather" bar, holding it ajar for Hayden to enter. As they stepped into the dimly lit establishment, the scent of polished wood and lingering notes of last night's spilled spirits greeted them. The interior boasted an air of curated sophistication, with black granite countertops reflecting the subtle glow of pendant lights above. Aged wooden tables, their surfaces etched with the memories of countless patrons, were haphazardly arranged across the worn hardwood floor.

The wallpaper, a tapestry of elaborate floral patterns entwined with mythical creatures, added a touch of whimsy to the otherwise austere decor. The place was closed for the morning, but a few employees were still sweeping the floors and cleaning tables, getting ready for the opening shift.

Hayden's gaze swept across the room, taking in the ambiance that Tessa had once been a part of. She could almost imagine the buzz of conversation, the clink of ice against glass, the ebb and flow of a typical evening crowd. But now, in the quiet aftermath, there was only the soft hum of a refrigerator and the occasional creak of a bar stool.

Advancing towards the bar with a measured stride, Hayden approached the lone figure still working behind it. The man was the human embodiment of the bar itself: timeless, sturdy, with a presence that suggested years of stories untold. His gray beard was neatly trimmed, and his rolled-up shirtsleeves revealed forearms mapped with veins and faded tattoos. He was wiping down the already spotless counter with a rag, his movements methodical and unhurried.

"Excuse me," Hayden said, her voice steady despite the uncertainty churning within her. "I'm looking for information about one of your former bartenders, Tessa."

The man paused mid-swipe, straightening up as he turned to regard her with eyes that had seen more than their fair share of human nature. There was a flicker of recognition, perhaps not for Tessa's name, but for the kind of conversation that was about to unfold – one that dug up the past and asked questions people often preferred to leave unasked.

"Ah, Tessa," he said, his voice a low rumble that seemed to reverberate through the quiet bar. "Didn't show up to work last night. I asked her to cover for me so I could go see my mom. Everyone loves her, but they don't know she's a total flake."

"You know," Hayden tells him, "she was found dead just yesterday."

"Dead?" he said, the blood draining from his face. "What? How? Did she get in a car wreck or something?"

"We're not at liberty to discuss that at this time," said Hayden, wanting to spare him the details. "But it is the subject of an investigation. Could you tell us a little more about her?"

The barkeeper leaned back against the counter, his gaze drifting upwards in thought. "Like I said, people loved her. Quick with a smile and quicker with the shaker," he mused, his voice tinged with respect. "Customers came for the drinks but stayed for her charm." His eyes met Hayden's again, steady and clear. "Why do you ask?"

"Was she into art?" Hayden inquired, trying to keep her tone casual, even though every fiber in her being was taut with the need for useful information.

"Art, huh?" He scratched his bearded chin, considering. "She doodled on napkins, made little sketches here and there. Some folks liked them enough to take home, but Tessa never made much fuss about it. It was just something she did to unwind, I reckon."

Hayden felt a twinge of disappointment. She'd hoped for a lead, something to connect the dots, but Tessa's life outside the bar remained a stubborn puzzle missing too many pieces.

"Thanks for your time," she said, giving the man a tight-lipped smile that didn't quite reach her eyes.

"Anytime, detective," he replied, nodding solemnly as if acknowledging the weight upon her shoulders.

Outside, the morning air was cool and sharp, a stark contrast to the dim warmth of the bar. Marcus was waiting for her, his expression etched with concern.

"Anything?" he asked.

"Dead end," Hayden responded, her frustration simmering beneath her calm exterior. "Let's split up. You head back to the office; I need some air to think."

Marcus studied her for a moment before nodding. "Alright, I'll see what else I can dig up. Call if you need anything."

Watching him walk away, Hayden's hands balled into fists at her sides. The case was gnawing at her, the lack of progress like a thorn in her side. She needed clarity, a fresh perspective, something to break through the fog of dead ends and silence.

Her feet moved with purpose as she navigated the streets, each step taking her closer to the familiar house that stood as a reservoir of wisdom in her tumultuous world. Dr. Simon Adler's home was an anchor, its sturdy brick facade and neatly trimmed hedges a testament to the order and insight she so desperately sought.

She raised her hand to the door, hesitating only a moment before rapping her knuckles against the wood. It was not long before the door swung open, revealing the kindly face of her old mentor, lines of age etched around kind eyes that had guided her more times than she could count.

"Dr. Adler," Hayden greeted, a semblance of relief washing over her as she stepped into the threshold of guidance she knew so well.

"Come in, Hayden," Dr. Adler said, stepping aside to allow her entry into his home. The warm light from inside spilled out onto the porch, enveloping her in a comforting glow that seemed at odds with the turmoil roiling within her.

As she entered, he closed the door behind her, shutting out the coolness of the outside world. She followed him through the corridor lined with bookshelves overflowing with wisdom accumulated over decades, their spines as familiar to her as the lines on her own hands.

They arrived at the kitchen, where the scent of mint and chamomile hinted at the herbal remedies that often accompanied their discussions.

"Sit down," he gestured towards the table while reaching for two mugs and a teapot adorned with an intricate pattern of vines and leaves. He poured the steaming liquid with a steady hand, the sound of the water hitting the ceramic a soothing background to the cacophony of thoughts in Hayden's head.

"Thank you," she murmured, wrapping her fingers around the mug. The heat seeped into her palms, grounding her as she tried to gather her scattered thoughts.

Dr. Adler took the seat opposite her, his gaze holding hers with the patience and concern of someone who had mentored many troubled souls. "Talk to me, Hayden. What brings you here seeking solace?"

Hayden took a sip of the tea, letting the warmth slide down her throat before speaking. "I need a fresh perspective, Simon. This case..." She trailed off, her mind flitting through the scant clues they had gathered so far. She explained what she could of the events so far.

"Art can be a window to the soul, but also a mirror reflecting our deepest obsessions," Dr. Adler mused, tapping his finger lightly on the table. "Consider the possibility that the killer has a passion for art, much like the victims. It might be the thread that draws them together."

"An artist himself, maybe?" Hayden pondered aloud, turning the idea over in her mind.

"Perhaps," Dr. Adler nodded, his voice measured. "Or simply an aficionado. But remember, sharing an interest in art could be how he locates his victims, not necessarily why he chooses to kill them. The 'why' is buried deeper, intertwined with emotions and psyche."

Hayden let the implication of his words sink in, feeling the beginnings of a new pathway forming in her investigation. The connection to art wasn't the motive; it was a method of selection, a way for the killer to identify with his prey before unraveling them thread by thread.

"Art is the common ground, but not the killing field," she said, a spark igniting behind her eyes. "That's where I need to look next."

"Exactly," Dr. Adler affirmed, his voice the guiding light she needed. "Find the link between their passions and his purpose."

She clutched the mug tighter, its warmth now a beacon of hope in the chilling puzzle laid out before her. With a renewed sense of direction, Hayden knew what she had to do.

CHAPTER TWENTY ONE

The dim lights of the Seattle Art Museum cast long shadows along the marble floors, cloaking him in darkness. He stood motionless, a predator blending into the environment. His heart thumped with a mix of adrenaline and nostalgia as he watched the last of the patrons trickle out, their murmurs and footsteps fading away. The killer, once an icon of artistry, now lurked like a specter where spotlights had once followed his every step.

He approached the back door, a relic from his celebrated past, and slid the keycard from his pocket. A soft beep broke the silence, and the lock disengaged with a click that resonated sweetly in his ears. Surprise flickered across his face, replaced quickly by a smug grin. No alarms sounded. No voices called out. He stepped through the threshold, invisible to all.

Slipping past the galleries where his masterpieces used to hang, once upon a time, he felt the cold scrutiny of the frames on the wall—judging, but silent.

He was once a welcome guest in places like this.

The service elevator doors opened with a reluctant groan, and he descended into the bowels of the building, leaving the world of exhibitions and accolades behind.

The basement was a stark contrast to the opulence above. Here, there were no velvet ropes, no sparkling champagne flutes raised in toast.

He remembered the days when he came to places like this to be photographed and swooned over. Journalists would hang on to his every word. People would offer enormous amounts of money just to commission a piece of his. He remembered the glittering lights, the way the patrons smiled at him, the way gallerists would clamor for his attention, eager to be part of his genius. But that adulation had faded, and the crowds had dispersed, leaving him to navigate the sterile corridors alone—a ghost haunting the catacombs of his former temple.

Now, in this place, he was just another forgotten ghost.

A name that sounded vaguely familiar but was quickly forgotten.

His footsteps echoed through the service area, a rhythmic reminder of his fall from grace. Where he had once been the artiste, the visionary, he was now just another shadow, indistinguishable from those who cleaned up after the museum closed. But he clung to the vestiges of his notoriety, the phantom applause still ringing in his ears, fueling his resolve for what had to be done next.

The hum of the ventilation system was a steady companion as he inched closer to where Bianca Morse was working. He could sense the concentration in the air, the dedication to her craft palpable even before he laid eyes on her. The best art restorer in Seattle, perhaps in the entire Pacific Northwest, and she was just around the corner, oblivious to his presence.

As he peered around the edge of the wall, he saw Bianca hunched over a large canvas, her hands moving with deft precision. A set of tiny vials lined up like soldiers beside her workbench, each containing a different solution meticulously crafted to restore ancient masterpieces to their former glory. She handled a dropper with the care of a surgeon, adding minute amounts of chemicals to a cotton swab before applying it to the painting's surface.

Watching her, he felt a momentary twinge—a memory of admiration for his own creations that once earned similar reverence.

It seemed like another lifetime when Bianca had looked at his pieces with wide-eyed wonder, praising the innovation, the emotion he poured into every stroke.

He remembered the conversations they'd had when she asked him what inspired his work, how he managed to blend so many mediums, how he wanted to be remembered as an artist.

Now he just wanted to be remembered at all.

Times had changed, and a newer artist had gotten her attention.

He had dedicated his life to the craft of painting, and in the end, it had all been for nothing.

But now, she was wholly engrossed in the restoration, her focus locked on brushing away centuries of grime to reveal the vibrant hues beneath. The Renaissance paintings under her care were being given a new lease on life, their original colors emerging like the sun breaking through the clouds.

He thought about the irony—how once she had been captivated by the contemporary art he'd wrought from nothing, and now her world was consumed by the painstaking resurrection of classics. His name, which used to be whispered in these halls with a mix of awe and envy, seemed to have dissolved, just like the accumulated dirt on those aged canvases under Bianca's expert touch.

Everything was different now. No admiration, no adulation—just the methodical swish of her hand, working to uncover the brilliance that time had obscured.

The silence of the museum was a stark contrast to the storm of rage brewing within him. He reached into his pack with a hand that trembled not from fear but from a barely contained fury. His fingers found the cloth, heavy with chloroform, and he clenched it tightly, as if gripping onto the last vestiges of his forgotten glory.

Stealthily, he navigated through the hall, his shadow melding with the others cast by the dim security lights. Ahead, the muffled beats of music pulsed through the air, a rhythmic thumping that masked the sound of his approach. Bianca, oblivious in her acoustic cocoon, continued her meticulous work, her headphones a barrier to the outside world.

His steps were silent, predatory, each one closing the distance between vengeance and its unsuspecting target. She was so close now that he could see the gentle bob of her head in time with the music, the delicate strands of hair that escaped her loose bun swaying hypnotically.

And then, with the precise timing of an artist delivering the final brush stroke, he struck. The rag swept through the air with a whisper, descending upon her just as she turned.

He tried to turn away, but in the darkly lit room, there was nowhere else to go.

Their eyes met for a heartbeat.

Fear surged through his veins. He thought about running away, but it was too late to back down. However, he'd lost his momentum, and without the usual element of surprise to hide behind, he froze.

She looked back at him, in as much shock as he was, too unnerved to scream for help.

In fact, she looked more confused than shocked. And the worst part was, there was no recognition on her face. No understanding who he was or why he was there.

"You don't remember me?" he growled, forgetting his initial fear. Because he thought this attack would be private and quick, he had opted not to cover his face. But he had a chloroform-soaked rag in one hand, ready to put her to sleep.

"Should I?" she asked. "I'm sorry. I'm very busy at the moment. Perhaps if you're here to clean the floors, you could do it another time?"

"Clean the floors?" he seethed. "There was a time when you would have given anything just for a glimpse inside my studio, and now, you're confusing me for the custodial staff?"

"I'm sorry, should I know you?" she asked. "It is kind of dark in here."

"You should know me anywhere. Everyone should. I should be a household name by now."

He took a step forward, and she began to back away slowly.

"They tell you that if you have talent, and you stick with it, then eventually you'll have success."

"Who is they?" she asked.

He took another step forward.

"They tell you that if you work hard enough and give art everything you have, then eventually, it will give you something back."

"You know, I really don't think…"

"But they lied. Art betrayed me. The world betrayed me. Used me for my talent and then forgot about me."

Then, her gaze filled with recognition, surprise, and something akin to betrayal.

"Oh, I do remember you. But my dear, you did have your moment in the sun."

"I did?" he asked, wondering if perhaps this meant that his work was more memorable than he thought it was.

"You did. And you wasted it. You didn't continue to improve your work. You spent all that money on expensive houses and more expensive vacations. I don't know what I thought happened to you, but cleaning the floors of a gallery wasn't too far off."

But before the emotions could fully paint themselves across her features, they were washed away by the chemical-induced darkness.

As she slumped to the ground, he caught her, lowering her limp form with a care that belied the violence of his act. A smug sense of satisfaction curled his lips upward. He had bested her, reclaimed a moment of dominion in this place that had once been his realm. Even as her consciousness waned, she had looked at him—truly seen him—and in that fleeting instance, he existed again, not as a relic of the past, but as the master of this current, dark canvas.

He knelt beside Bianca's still form, the vial of arsenic in his hand glinting coldly under the harsh basement lights.

Rage surged through his blood.

He would show her the truth.

He hadn't wasted his moment. In fact, his best work was yet to come.

His fingers, once praised for their ability to coax life onto canvas, now trembled with a different anticipation. The poison was a silent partner to his wrath, a mere whisper away from quieting the dissonant chords within him.

With meticulous care, he prepared to administer the lethal substance, reveling in the control that had long eluded him. He leaned forward, the vial poised, his breath a soft hiss against the silence. But then, the faint echo of a footstep in the stairwell stabbed the quiet, splintering his focus.

His head snapped toward the sound, eyes narrowing. Time, suddenly an enemy, hastened its pace, and his heart pounded a frenzied rhythm against his ribs. The old sensation of being watched, hunted even in his own sanctuary, crept up on him. He had to move—now.

With a swiftness born of necessity, he pocketed the vial and scooped Bianca into his arms. She was feather-light, her body limp, a marionette with severed strings. He half-carried, half-dragged her across the cool concrete floor, each step a calculated risk.

The freight elevator, a boxy relic that once carried his masterpieces to light, loomed ahead—a gateway to his escape. He maneuvered Bianca's unconscious form through the wide doors, laying her down just as they lumbered closed with an echoing thud.

As the elevator jolted upwards, the sounds from the stairwell grew louder, more insistent. Footsteps paired with the crackle of a walkie-talkie, the static-laden voice of a museum security guard cutting through the tension. The guard rounded the corner, flashlight beam sweeping across the room like a lighthouse in search of shipwrecks, just a heartbeat too late.

Hidden within the elevator's metal carcass, he exhaled, the close call igniting a flare of adrenaline that coursed through his veins. Though thwarted, he felt the thrill of the chase, the sweet satisfaction of evading capture. As the elevator ascended, he stood watch over Bianca, a fallen angel in his darkened purgatory, while the shadows of the Seattle Art Museum swallowed them whole.

CHAPTER TWENTY TWO

The steering wheel felt cold and unyielding under Hayden's grip, much like the case that had burrowed its way under her skin. As she navigated the familiar bends leading back to the field office, the words of Adler echoed in the confines of her car, each syllable bouncing around with a weight that demanded consideration. Art. The very word painted strokes of insight across her mind's canvas. Could the passion for such beauty be perverted into a motive for murder?

Her gaze flickered to the passing scenery, but her focus was inward, probing at the idea that the killer might be driven not by the message but by a twisted love for the medium itself. The notion settled uneasily within her, a piece of a puzzle that was gradually forming an unsettling picture.

Pulling into the parking lot, Hayden killed the engine and took a moment to steady her breath. She knew that understanding the killer's affinity for art could be key to unraveling the mystery, yet it also broadened the suspect pool to an almost unmanageable degree. With a determined exhale, she stepped out into the crisp air, squaring her shoulders against the burden of the unsolved crimes.

The field office hummed with the low buzz of fluorescent lights and the quiet tap of keyboards. Marcus was hunched over his desk, his eyes scanning lines of data that seemed as fruitless in their search as they were exhaustive. His dedication was a constant, a beacon in the chaos of their work, and seeing him so immersed provided Hayden with a jolt of purpose.

"Any luck on the arsenic angle?" she asked, approaching the desk with a tiredness that only another long day could bring.

Marcus glanced up, his expression etched with the frustration of dead ends and false leads. "I've been combing through every purchase and supplier within a fifty-mile radius," he said, rubbing the bridge of his nose wearily. "But it's like looking for a needle in a haystack made of needles."

Hayden's heart sank. She had braced herself for this outcome, yet hope had been a stubborn companion. "So, we're back to square one," she muttered, feeling the leaden weight of uncertainty tug at her resolve.

"Looks that way," Marcus conceded, pushing his chair back and standing with the slow creak of bones that had seen too many hours at a desk. "Unless we can find a more specific link to the art world, we might as well be chasing shadows."

"Then that's what we'll do," Hayden replied, the gears in her mind already turning with renewed determination. "We'll chase those shadows until they bleed daylight, Marcus. There's a connection here, and I'm going to find it." She returned to her car in a hurry.

Hayden's fingers tapped a staccato rhythm against the steering wheel as she sat in her car and navigated the crowded digital archives on her tablet, the glow of the screen casting stark shadows across her focused features. Then, her eyes were snagged by a name that leaped out from the list of local artists associated with the community center: Clifton York.

"York," she murmured, rolling the name around in her mind like a puzzle piece, searching for its fit. She jotted it down in her notepad, a tangible reminder. With a decisive swipe, Hayden delved deeper, tracing York's artistic footprints through cyberspace until she landed on an Op-Ed from a recent newspaper.

The headline was bold, almost aggressive in its assertion: "A Dark Turn: The Unnerving Evolution of Clifton York." The article painted a vivid picture of an artist whose palette had shifted from vibrant to somber, his themes increasingly macabre. Intrigued, Hayden leaned back in her seat, absorbing the words that described how York's latest series left viewers unsettled, the canvases imbued with an intensity that bordered on the sinister.

"Interesting," Hayden conceded with a thoughtful frown, but she wasn't ready to slip the noose of suspicion around York's neck just yet. Darkness in art did not a killer make, and she was wary of conflating creative expression with criminal intent.

Still, something nagged at her—a professional itch that demanded she follow every lead, no matter how tenuous. With a few more taps, Hayden found herself on Clifton York's website, the virtual gallery a stark contrast to the drab interior of her car.

His work was a cacophony of color and chaos, each painting a visual shout that seemed to dare the observer to look away. Hayden scrolled through the images, drawn in despite herself. York's style was brash, unapologetically avant-garde, and completely at odds with the sterile environment of her daily grind. It was easy to see why he had gained notoriety; there was an undeniable magnetism to the raw, almost primal energy of his work.

"Maybe too easy," she whispered, her admiration tinged with the skepticism that was her constant companion. Hayden took a moment more to study the paintings, looking for the unseen thread that might connect York to their case. But appreciation of his artistry offered no clarity on his innocence or guilt.

Her mind was abuzz with possibilities, but without concrete evidence, they were nothing more than conjecture. She'd need more than a thematic shift in an artist's oeuvre to build a case, and so the hunt would continue.

"Let's hope you're just a painter, Mr. York," she said to the screen. Then, squaring her shoulders, she headed back into the building, ready to sift through reality's gray tones in search of the black-and-white truth.

Hayden leaned forward at her desk now, her eyes narrowing as she scrolled through the digital gallery on Clifton York's website. The familiarity of a particular style—a distinctive brushstroke—tugged at the edge of her memory. She paused on a portrait, its bold colors and aggressive lines clamoring for attention. The subject's eyes, a piercing blue, seemed to stare directly into hers. It was Laura.

"Of course," Hayden muttered under her breath, a flash of recognition igniting in her mind. She flicked to the next painting, and there was Erica, depicted with the same intensity, the same unsettling gaze that reached out from the canvas. York wasn't just some local artist; he was the name on everyone's lips when they spoke of the avant-garde art scene in the area. How had she missed this connection?

"Marcus," she looked over at her partner, tapping the screen of her tablet to show him the portraits. "Look at this."

Marcus swiveled in his chair, eyebrows knitting together as he took in the images. "That's... unexpected," he said, leaning back. His hand rubbed at the stubble on his chin thoughtfully. "Laura and Erica, huh?"

"Exactly. They must've modeled for him." The shock was still fresh on Hayden's face, the pieces of the puzzle coming together yet leaving gaping holes. "But why didn't we know about it until now?"

"Let's see if they were compensated," Marcus suggested, already pulling up their financial records on his computer. Minutes ticked by and the only sound between them was the click of keys and the occasional frustrated sigh.

"Nothing," Hayden declared after a thorough search, her expression growing stormier. "No transactions, no official credits on his site. They're practically ghosts."

"Looks like they might have been paid off the books," Marcus concurred, turning to face her. "We need to figure out why."

Hayden's mind raced with implications, each one more troubling than the last. She knew they were onto something—the absence of evidence was telling. But without solid proof, they were grasping at shadows. Determination set her jaw firm as she stepped away from Marcus's desk, her resolve hardening.

"Let's keep digging," she said, her voice steady despite the whirlwind of thoughts. They had uncovered a new lead, a thread in the dark tapestry of their case. Now it was time to unravel it.

Hayden stood, the chair scraping softly against the floor of the field office. Marcus had already begun to gather his notes, a silent agreement hanging between them that the next step was unavoidable. Her eyes met his briefly, and she saw the same steely resolve reflected there.

"We need to talk to Clifton York," she stated, her voice carrying an edge of command.

"Agreed," Marcus replied, pushing back from his desk. "He might have answers about the other victims too. It's not just Laura and Erica anymore."

"Exactly." Hayden reached for her blazer draped over the back of her chair, the fabric cool and smooth under her fingers. It felt like donning armor, a necessary shield for the confrontation ahead.

Marcus's hand paused on his notepad, his brows knitting together in thought. "If he paid them under the table, there could be more to their relationship than just artist and muse," he mused aloud, echoing the worry clawing at the back of Hayden's mind.

"Which means he could be the connection we've been looking for," Hayden finished, her thoughts aligning with his. The silence that followed was heavy with implication.

She dug a little deeper into York's business dealings on her phone and found that he owed the IRS a notable amount of back taxes. He was flat broke.

Maybe he blamed the victims for his financial downfall.

The air in the room seemed to thrum with the potential of the lead they were about to follow. With a determined nod, she gestured towards the door. "Let's go."

The corridor outside Marcus's office felt colder than Hayden remembered, a chill that seeped through her clothes and raised goosebumps along her arms. She ignored it, focusing instead on the growing sense of anticipation. Each step toward the exit was purposeful, the weight of her gun at her hip a constant reminder of the stakes.

As they passed through the sliding glass doors of the field office, the late afternoon sun cast long shadows across the parking lot. Hayden squinted against the glare, her mind already racing ahead to the encounter with York. Could this enigmatic artist hold the key to unlocking the entire mystery?

She slid behind the wheel of the unmarked sedan, the familiar scent of leather and stale coffee greeting her. Marcus settled into the passenger seat, flipping open his notepad to a clean page, ready to jot down any new information.

"Clifton York," Hayden murmured to herself as the engine roared to life beneath her hands. The words felt like a puzzle piece clicking into place, yet the picture was still incomplete.

She glanced over at Marcus, noting the firm set of his jaw, the way his eyes narrowed with focus. They were partners in this tangled web, each relying on the other's strengths.

"Let's hope he's our man," Marcus said, his voice low but firm.

"Hope isn't a strategy," Hayden replied, though her heart echoed his sentiment. She put the car in gear, the tires crunching over the gravel as they began their journey towards truth—or another dead end.

But as the field office disappeared in the rearview mirror, Hayden allowed herself a sliver of hope. This could be it—the breakthrough they needed to bring a killer to justice and close a case that had haunted her for far too long.

CHAPTER TWENTY THREE

Hayden had looked thoroughly into her next suspect, who she felt a cautiously hopeful about. The more she looked into his life, the more he fit the profile of the person she was searching for.

Clifton York, the elusive artist with a penchant for seclusion, seemed as tangible as a wisp of smoke. She had scoured social media, acquaintances, even researched his last known address — all for naught.

By all accounts, he had been a thing of the past for several years after a promising start as a young artist. According to a piece in a small art magazine, he had dazzled a few important critics early on with mixed media and elaborate painting. He even made enough to buy a few houses in fancy locations, run a studio in Paris, take models on sailing trips to the Virgin Islands.

And then, all of a sudden, his popularity faded.

Artists with a longer track record resurfaced. His work started to lose its value, and his new paintings were nothing more than repeats of the old ones. Unable to break out of a stroke of bad luck, he faded into the background, as good as blackballed from any major gallery or museum. He only appeared in the news because of a rather high-profile divorce, where his wife accused him of cheating with several of his models.

Hayden remembered another reason why she hadn't gone into art as a career.

Her heart was with helping the victims of crimes, but she also knew that the art world was fickle as the wind. One moment, you were the darling of every collector in the country, the next minute you were a has-been washout waiting to catch another big break.

And this out of luck artist didn't have much of a habit of paying bills for housing, keeping phone records, or having any kind of permanent address.

They had looked everywhere, but his previous properties had been foreclosed on.

It was Marcus, skimming through a directory of local art studios, who struck gold.

"Got him," Marcus said, pointing to a scribbled note on the margin of the page. "A mutual friend mentioned Clifton's been crashing at his studio while he's out of town. Apparently, it's a popular spot for people in the art world."

"A studio," Hayden echoed.

"Of course. He'd blend in at any studio. Especially if he's looking for a way back into the art scene."

With a sense of purpose renewing her focus, Hayden navigated to the new location. She waited impatiently as the traffic slowed down their journey.

They drove in silence, the cityscape a blur of color and motion outside the windows.

Hayden made note of the street cameras that they passed, hoping that if he had a weak alibi, she could look into when his car was seen coming and going.

Upon arrival, the studio door creaked open, betraying its frequent use.

The scent of paint and clay greeted Hayden, tugging at a seldom-acknowledged desire nestled deep within her chest. Artists, real artists, had always held a certain allure. She knew that a messy lifestyle and living space was a part of the charm. She wasn't exactly neat herself.

Their world was one where passion bled into every stroke, every sculpture, every photograph. A twinge of jealousy pricked her conscience, a reminder of dreams deferred in the pursuit of law and order.

"Smells like creativity," Marcus murmured, pulling her from her reverie.

"Smells like trouble," she countered softly, thinking of the darkness that so often lurked beneath the surface of beauty. The art world was no stranger to scandal, and their quarry was proof enough that brilliance did not preclude a person from sinister deeds.

They stepped further inside, the air thick with the mustiness of clay and the acrid tang of oils, each breath drawing them deeper into Clifton York's domain.

Hayden's eyes adjusted to the studio's uneven light, her gaze landing on Clifton York. He stood, solitary, before a canvas splashed with hues that spoke of tragedy. The subject was a doe, its form rendered in jarring multimedia contrasts—the fragility of life captured in the stillness of death on the side of a road. Hayden felt the raw edge of emotion in the piece, yet it eluded her grasp, the meaning as cryptic as a cipher.

"Mr. York?" she called out, her voice slicing through the hush of concentration.

Clifton didn't start; he merely turned his head slightly, acknowledging their presence. His eyes had the detached focus of a man who lived more in the world of his creations than in reality. "What is it?"

"We just need a moment of your time," Hayden said, her detective's mind trying to bridge the gap between her appreciation for art and the enigma of the artist before her.

"Can't you see I'm working?" There was a note of irritation in his voice, dismissive and weary. "I don't converse. I don't eat. Not while I'm in this space." He gestured vaguely at the air around him, as if it were filled with invisible threads only, he could sense.

Hayden looked up at a painting with a dark color and a grotesque theme emerging from the vague shapes.

"Your work can wait just a few minutes," Hayden insisted, her patience wearing thin against his aloof demeanor. She needed answers, and this man, lost in his own abstract world, held them like a reluctant muse.

Hayden stepped closer to the canvas, the smell of paint and turpentine thick in her nostrils. Clifton's brush continued to dance across the surface, a defiant act against the interruption.

"Whoever you want to talk about, I'm sure it will only distract me. And I don't have time for distractions."

"We've noticed that your work has been less popular than it used to be, Mr. York," said Marcus.

"Didn't realize that police were investigating trends in the fine art world," he said.

"How did you…" Hayden began. They hadn't announced themselves as detectives.

"It is my job to see things, my dear," he said, without looking back over his shoulder.

"Actually, we're FBI," Marcus corrected, showing his badge.

"Close enough," he said.

"Then maybe you'll humor us and answer the question."

Clifton sighed. "I know that a lot of people find this hard to believe, but I actually don't care if my art holds its value or not. I paint because

I must paint. What the critics and gallerists say about it on any particular day isn't within my control."

Hayden couldn't help but respect this answer. But she was still suspicious.

"We noticed that you were recently foreclosed on and went through a rather expensive divorce," Hayden said. "That had to have been stressful."

"Is there a crime here, agents?"

"Just questions."

"Look, I am not exactly good at making financial decisions. I spent a little faster than I should have. Had to pull back a bit."

She nodded, not knowing what to believe. Moments before, she had been so certain that they'd found the right guy. Now, she was beginning to doubt herself.

"Clifton, I need to discuss Laura and Erica with you," she said firmly, her gaze locked onto his profile as he worked. She saw the slight clench of his jaw at the mention of the names but nothing more; his expression remained impassive.

"They both modeled in your work."

With an abrupt cessation of movement, he laid his brush down and turned to face her.

"Erica and Laura," he scoffed, the words dripping with disdain. "What about them?"

"Did you know them well?"

"I suppose. Of course, I wasn't the only one who painted them."

"But you did know them," pressed Marcus.

"Past tense? Is that what this is about? Did something happen to them?"

Neither one of them answered.

"They were mistakes—blemishes on my body of work."

Hayden observed him carefully, noting the curl of his lip as he spoke of the two women. There was resentment there, something deeper than mere artistic critique.

"Those paintings are my worst," Clifton continued, his voice rising slightly with a mix of anger and regret. "Had I never painted those two, my entire collection would be esteemed at double its value. They brought nothing but ruin to my art."

Hayden's eyes narrowed, reading between the lines of his vehement denunciation. It was clear that whatever relationship Clifton York had with Erica and Laura, it had soured to the point of complete repudiation.

"Clifton, what about Naomi Cruz and Tessa Rodriguez? Any connection to them?" Hayden pressed, her eyes searching his for a flicker of recognition or guilt.

"They're just faces in the crowd," Clifton replied with a shrug, his voice carrying an airy indifference. "Petals on a wet, black bow."

Hayden's brow furrowed. “What does that mean?”

“It’s Pound. Ezra Pound. Sort of.”

Hayden raised an eyebrow.

“I haven’t heard those names before, no,” he said, more clearly. “But I don’t learn the names of everyone I meet.”

"And where were you on the nights in question?"

“Which nights would those be, agents?”

“The last two nights, of course,” said Hayden.

"Here," he gestured vaguely at the cluttered studio, "immersed in my work. I don't step out; I don't entertain. Solitude is my only companion."

Marcus stepped forward, his patience clearly worn down by the evasive answers. "No one to vouch for your whereabouts? You have a reason to dislike two of the victims. That's not looking good for you, Clifton."

“I guess not,” he said.

“One last question. Do you ever use arsenic in your paint?”

“A lot of people do,” he said.

“Clifton York, you’re under arrest,” Marcus said.

As he announced it, Hayden wasn’t sure it was the right call. Sure, he was suspicious, but there had to be more than one down on their luck artist in their town.

"Arresting me on what grounds?" Clifton's voice held a mocking tone, but there was a slight tremor in his hands now.

"Obstruction and suspicion of involvement," Marcus declared as he took out his handcuffs. "You have the right to remain silent..."

Hayden watched as Marcus methodically secured Clifton's wrists, noting the rigid way Clifton held himself, as if still in defiance of the situation unfolding around him. The scent of paint and clay was now laced with a tension that seemed to seep into the very walls of the studio.

They guided Clifton outside, the evening air feeling abrupt and cool after the stuffy interior. Hayden slid into the driver's seat, her mind racing as they drove toward the station. Clifton sat quietly in the back, his face inscrutable in the rearview mirror.

The silence was soon filled with the hum of the engine and Hayden's thoughts. She recalled the images from the crime scenes – elaborate, almost Baroque in their horror, a stark contrast to the minimalist lines and sparse compositions that characterized Clifton's art.

She thought about the crime scenes compared to his actual art.

His work was abstract and minimalist... nothing like the maximalist crime scenes.

Marcus met her eyes, a shared uncertainty passing between them as the car sped on through the darkening streets. Clifton remained silent, an enigma trapped within his own cryptic world of color and shape.

CHAPTER TWENTY FOUR

Hayden's fingers traced the contours of inked lines sprawling across the pages taped to the conference room wall, each a meticulous reconstruction of the crime scenes that had haunted her waking hours. The field office buzzed beyond the glass panes, a hive of agents in motion, but within this space, silence loomed heavy as she and Marcus faced the mute defiance of Clifton's sketches.

She had gone back over Clifton's work and noticed a dark turn that each of his paintings had taken recently.

But even though he seemed guilty and didn't have a good alibi, something about the whole thing didn't sit right.

He didn't seem to have much need for revenge. He said himself that he didn't care what his paintings sold for, and he wasn't particularly stressed about not having his own place to live.

"Lawyer is on his way," Marcus grumbled, dropping into one of the chairs with a sigh that seemed to carry the weight of their stalled investigation. "Won't talk, won't even look at us. Like we're beneath him."

"Clifton seems to think that this whole investigation is beneath him," Hayden murmured, eyes never leaving the drawings. "Like his art is the only thing in the world that matters."

"Yeah," agreed Marcus. "Except in this case, life imitates art. Or death rather."

Hayden shuddered at the thought.

Her finger paused on a line too bold, a shadow too dramatic for the minimalist hand they suspected.

"His work is a study in understatement—deliberation in every dot and stroke." She stepped back, arms crossed as she considered the evidence sprawled before them. "This..." She shook her head slowly, looking back at the crime scene renderings. Most of Clifton's paintings were monochromatic, distant, vague shapes, like shadows in the mist. But the crime scenes made use of things like beading, jewelry, even a dead animal. That screamed maximalism.

"This is grandiose, an homage to a time when art was meant to be anything but subtle."

Marcus leaned forward, forearms resting on his knees, his gaze sharpening as he followed her train of thought.

“I don’t follow.”

"Artists tend to have a particular style. Clifton has stuck to the same minimalism for his whole career. His paintings are abstract and simple, even though they've gotten darker recently. But the killer doesn't seem to like minimalism. It isn't a style used in any of the paintings that he's mimicking, and he's added things to the crime scenes to make them more elaborate," she explained.

"So, what are you saying? The styles don’t match?" She could hear a hint of frustration in his voice.

"Exactly." Hayden turned, her eyes alight with the spark of intuition that had made her reputation. "The killer's not just killing; he's communicating. And he's using a language Clifton would never deign to speak. Plagiarism is beneath him—crude mimicry doubly so."

"An artist's pride," Marcus muttered, nodding in agreement.

"More than that," Hayden added, a determined edge to her voice. "It's his identity. To copy is to admit defeat, to concede that someone else's vision surpasses your own. Clifton doesn’t copy. None of his previous paintings pay homage to his predecessors."

“Okay,” Marcus said. “Don’t tell me this brings us back to square one.”

Hayden shook her head. “No, this helps us understand the case much better. We can wait for York’s lawyer, and then keep looking for other leads, ones that might fit the profile a little bit better. If we do interrogate Clifton, we still might find that he’s guilty. But in the meantime, I think that it’s best to investigate all possibilities.”

"Well, let’s do it then." Marcus’s tone held a note of frustration, but his eyes were thoughtful, considering the challenge anew. However, they wouldn’t be good detectives if they couldn’t put their personal feelings and frustrations about the case aside.

Marcus exhaled, a sound like surrender. "We keep hitting dead ends. Where do we even start looking for a new suspect?"

"Think about it," Hayden said, tapping a finger against her temple. "Clifton's models—they sat for him without leaving a trace. No paperwork, no official appointments. If they did it for him, they might've done it for someone else. He even mentioned that they modeled for others, so we need to find out who."

"Other artists," Marcus murmured, his skepticism gradually giving way to cautious optimism.

"Exactly. We can look into artists who have a style that matches the crime scene a little more closely. It's not an exact indicator, but it's a start." Hayden's voice was now a determined hum as she swiveled in her chair and booted up her laptop. The conference room felt suddenly too small, the air charged with potential. Her fingers flew across the keyboard, alighting on social media icons, typing in search queries with precision.

"Wait," Marcus interjected, leaning over her shoulder. "You think you can just find our guy through social media?"

"Watch me," Hayden replied, her eyes not leaving the screen. As far as she was concerned, social media was the best invention for people in law enforcement. Instead of digging for information that used to take hours or days to get access to, now people posted it themselves right to the internet.

Rather than searching through dozens of galleries in person, or even calling and asking for images of their portraits, she could find the work of local artists posted online in an attempt to gain the interest of more people buying artwork.

She navigated through profiles and pages, the light from the monitor casting an ever-changing glow on her face. Images of art and snippets of artist bios flickered by in rapid succession.

"Here," she said, pausing on a gallery of digital thumbnails. Each image portrayed a woman, her likeness captured in varying styles and strokes. Hayden's heart quickened; the faces bore a striking resemblance to the four victims.

"Those eyes," Marcus pointed to one portrait, his voice low with realization. "They're Tessa's."

"Gotcha," Hayden whispered, leaning closer as if the pixels could come alive and confirm her suspicions. She clicked through to the artist's profile, her mind piecing together a new narrative—one that wove through the fabric of brushwork and into the dark folds of motive and opportunity.

Hayden's eyes darted across the gleaming screen, tracing the breadcrumbs of digital footprints left behind by Laura and Naomi. Her pulse thrummed in her temples as she clicked on a tagged location, an artist's studio nestled within the web of social media. The page loaded, revealing the virtual showcase of one Ivan Markovic.

"Marcus," Hayden breathed, hardly containing the buzz of discovery under her skin. "Look at this."

The room shrank around them, the walls papered with Hayden's meticulous drawings, now bystanders to the unraveling thread of truth. Marcus stepped beside her, his gaze following her cursor as it hovered over a collection of portraits for sale. Each brushstroke on the canvas mirrored the contours and expressions of the women they sought to bring justice to, including Tessa.

"Is that...?" Marcus trailed off, needing no answer.

"It's them," Hayden confirmed, clicking through each portrait with growing conviction. "Laura, Naomi, all of them, immortalized by Ivan Markovic."

The resonance of the name hung between them, a clue crystallizing into a lead. Hayden delved deeper, her mind hungry for context, for history. A quick search unearthed articles from a decade past, whispers of fame that clung to Ivan like shadows to light. The MET, the pinnacle of artistic achievement, had once celebrated his work—a maximalist explosion of color and reference.

"Remember this?" Hayden asked, her voice tinged with nostalgia as she scanned an article detailing Ivan's success. "His painting in the MET was all anyone talked about back then."

Marcus nodded, the memory unspooling in his own recollection. But the past glory seemed distant now, the luster dimmed by the fickleness of art trends. As Hayden read on, the story shifted, the maximalism that had catapulted Ivan to stardom now a relic of yesteryear, abandoned by the ever-changing appetites of the art world.

"His style fell out of vogue," she said quietly, the realization settling like dust in the corners of their investigation.

With every click, every scroll, the picture of Ivan Markovic became clearer—his rise, his fall, the possibility of his connection to their case. Hayden leaned back, her eyes never leaving the screen, as the gears of her mind turned with relentless purpose.

Hayden's fingers hovered over the keyboard, a symphony of clicks filling the silence as she sifted through digital archives. A headline caught her eye, and she leaned in closer, absorbing the words that painted a portrait of desolation: "Local Artist's Parisian Dream Crumbles." The article narrated Ivan Markovic's financial ruin, detailing his lavish expenditure on a grandiose Paris residence, an investment that soon morphed into a sinkhole. The image of a forlorn mansion glared back at her from the screen, its opulence contrasting with the stark reality of a dream deferred.

"Marcus, look at this," Hayden murmured, beckoning him over. Her colleague rounded the table, peering down at the grainy photograph of Ivan standing before the ornate iron gates of his ill-fated home—a symbol of ambition outstripping grasp.

"Must've hit him hard, coming back to find the world had moved on," Marcus noted, his voice low, a thread of empathy woven through the words.

"Exactly," Hayden replied, her gaze not leaving the monitor. Her mind raced, piecing together the mosaic of Ivan's life. It wasn't just the art scene's cruel abandonment; it was personal, visceral. An idea started to form, a hypothesis that sent a chill down her spine.

"Could he be blaming these women for his downfall?" she pondered aloud. "The models—his muses—were emblems of his success. When they moved on, perhaps in his mind, they took his relevance with them."

Marcus nodded, processing the gravity of her suggestion. Hayden's eyes darted back to the search results, desperate for an address, a location, anything tangible. And then, like a lighthouse cutting through fog, there it was—an old interview mentioning Ivan's return to Seattle, complete with a mention of his studio tucked away in the industrial district.

"Got it!" she exclaimed, her pulse quickening. She scribbled down the address, her hand barely able to keep up with the urgency coursing through her veins. This was it—the lead they needed. She grabbed her jacket from the back of her chair, her movements practiced and precise.

"Where are you going?" Marcus asked, though the answer was clear in Hayden's determined set of her jaw.

"To his studio. If he's there, we need to talk to him before he has a chance to vanish again. We're running out of time."

"Wait for back-up," Marcus cautioned, but Hayden was already at the door, her resolve as unyielding as the truth she sought.

"Every second counts," she called back, not waiting for a response. The door shut behind her with a click that echoed her earlier typing, a final punctuation mark on the decision made. She headed for her car, the Seattle streets a blur as she navigated toward the address that might hold the key to everything—the unraveling of Ivan Markovic's tangled web.

CHAPTER TWENTY FIVE

Ivan's hands trembled, the weight of his revelation as heavy as the palette knife he'd set aside. The studio, once a sanctuary of creation, now felt like a foreign land, its corners shrouded with the dark reality of what he had become. He'd never imagined a scenario where his muses would need to be silenced permanently, but there she was—Bianca, his unintended captive, stirring back to consciousness in the dim light that filtered through the dirt-specked windows.

"Wh-why?" Bianca's voice was weak, but it pierced the silence like a chisel to marble. Her wrists were bound, her figure slumped against the cool concrete wall that bore witness to countless hours of Ivan's artistic fervor.

She looked up at him, her eyes searching for an answer.

He couldn't keep his thoughts straight. Bringing her here had not been a part of the plan. He wasn't prepared for it.

He paced back and forth.

"I already told you why," he growled. He just needed a moment of quiet to think about all of it, to find a way out. Of course, he already had the perfect place planned for her body. But now he had to figure out how to get her there.

"Ivan," she continued, a hint of disbelief lacing her words, "you were always so gentle, so dedicated to your art. I remember posing right here, feeling like part of something beautiful. Your work was good, truly."

"Don't lie," he said. "You made it clear what you really think of me at the museum."

She had quickly changed her tune after he kidnapped her, trying to flatter him. She said things like, "Your work is better than I remember. I have you confused with someone else." His favorite was, "This will all make a really interesting interview one day, when you make your big debut."

But he was done with any hope of returning to the art world. Instead, he vowed to punish it.

Her gaze fell upon a half-finished canvas, one that held the promise of Ivan's talent. She had seen his passion, watched as vibrant strokes of paint came alive beneath his deft touch.

"Please," she implored, her gaze unwavering, "I know that you've been down on your luck. I know the market for fine art is fickle. Just think about what happened to Van Gogh."

"Nothing happened to him," said Ivan. "He died in obscurity, just like I will."

"And how wrong the world was. You see? None of this is objective."

He huffed and continued to pace. None of it made him feel better.

"People come back from terrible falls all the time. Just sell one painting. It only takes one to turn it all around. It will make the value of your other work go up. You can get into galleries again. You can still make it as an artist without... without this."

The plea hung in the air, mingling with the scent of linseed oil and turpentine—a bitter reminder of a career teetering on the edge of oblivion. She wanted desperately to survive this and was offering anything she had to give just to have a chance.

"How about this? I'll buy one of your paintings. I'll put it in my friend's gallery, and we'll have you there to talk about it to potential collectors and critics. How does that sound?"

Ivan's breath hitched, caught between the man he once was and the one he had become. His vision blurred as he looked at Bianca, seeing not just the woman before him, but the embodiment of all his hopes and failures wrapped in flesh and bone.

"You're lying," he said. "The moment I let you go, you'll call the police."

"I won't. I promise."

"I know you're lying," he roared.

He swallowed hard, the tightness in his chest a cruel mimicry of the creative block that had haunted him for too long. Could one painting, one sale, rekindle the spark that once set his world ablaze? Or was he too far gone, lost in a labyrinth of his own making, where the exit was nothing more than a macabre masterpiece waiting to be crafted by his hand?

"Please—"

"Quiet!" Ivan's voice erupted through the studio, a harsh contrast to the gentle whispers that once danced around his canvases. The word was a bullet, shot from a place of darkness within him, and it ricocheted off the walls, off the eviscerated paintings, off the dust-laden windows.

His chest heaved, each breath a burden, as if he were trying to inhale the very inspiration that had forsaken him. There was no solace in the silence that followed; it was filled with the echoes of abandonment—by the world of art, by the muses, by Bianca and the other models whose features he once captured so lovingly. With every dismissal, every gallery door that closed on him, a piece of his spirit crumbled away.

"Abandoned," he muttered to himself, a mantra of betrayal. He began to pace, his movements erratic, like a caged animal. His footsteps were the only sound, pattering against the concrete floor, leading him in a frenzied circuit from the unkempt bed shoved in the corner to the kitchenette that bore witness to many a midnight oil burned in vain.

"Wrong! All wrong!" The words slipped out between gritted teeth. His eyes darted across the barren walls, where shadows played tricks, making him see grandeur where there was none. The room seemed to close in around him, suffocating, as if rejecting the presence of his maddening despair.

"Art abandoned me when I needed it most, even after I gave it everything."

"I'm sure that's not true," she said. "It's never too late."

"No," he said. "Maybe you should be more worried about yourself than me. The others were easier. Didn't put up a fight. Didn't wake up."

"You don't mean that you're the one who has been hurting people?" she asked.

"The others, they were just the beginning of a new series that I have been working on, paying homage to the greats."

"I saw in the news…" she had a blank, shocked look on her face. Her eyes went glassy.

"Would you like to know which painting I've had picked out for you?

Bianca... his supposed masterpiece, now just another symbol of his ruin. She was meant to be the one, the canvas that would reignite the art world's love for his work, the subject of his defining triumph. Yet here she lay, in this mausoleum of his aspirations, a place unfit for creation, let alone the birth of a magnum opus.

His hands shook as he paused, standing still for a moment as the realization clawed at his insides. This wasn't the sacred space of an artist—the temple where masterpieces were conceived. It was a tomb, cold and hollow, and he was its keeper, presiding over the death of his own dreams.

Ivan halted, a sudden stillness overtaking his previously erratic movements. His gaze shifted from the chaotic disarray of his studio to the delicate form of Bianca, her eyes reflecting the softness and vulnerability that had once inspired countless strokes of his brush. She was the embodiment of romantic sensibilities, her sensitivity a stark contrast to the harsh reality that now ensnared them both.

A whisper of an idea began to take shape in his fevered mind, growing clearer with each shallow breath he drew.

"Boreas," he murmured, the name of the ancient god of the North Wind evoking visions of untamed beauty and raw power. The very thought seemed to ignite a spark within him; it was perfect. He would model her after Boreas—wild, commanding, yet tragically beautiful. The last of the arsenic would be his medium, transforming flesh into eternal art.

"Please, Ivan," Bianca's voice cut through his reverie, her plea wrapped in unmistakable fear. Her words trembled in the air, "You don't need to do this. You don't have to hurt anyone anymore."

He turned toward her, his eyes darkened by the depth of his obsession. In his mind, there was no turning back, no other path but forward through the abyss he'd willingly plunged into. The point of no return had been crossed long ago, and now there was only the inexorable pull towards what he believed to be his destiny.

"Too late," he whispered, more to himself than to her, as he shuffled through the clutter of his broken dreams, searching for the vile instrument of his twisted salvation.

She set her teeth, a look of fury passing over her face.

"Fine!" she said, with a sudden fever that didn't seem to fit with someone who had been captured. "You want to know what I really think about your art, Ivan?"

“I think you’ve already made that clear.”

“Well, you’re going to hear a refresher anyway. Because your work was always derivative. An imitation of a better artist. Even when you’re killing people, you can’t come up with your own technique. And even if you do manage to kill me, they’ll track you down quickly. Because you can always tell a forgery from the real thing.

Ivan's gaze locked onto Bianca, the dim light casting shadows across her bound form.

His blood boiled with rage. Who was she to tell him how his own work should look? Who was she to judge the way that he had taken life?

He saw the references to art in each crime scene like a hat tip, a way of honoring those who had inspired him the most.

But even that decision was sneered at.

A perverse sense of clarity washed over him as he straightened his spine and took a step closer. His voice was steady, almost serene, as though he were discussing the weather rather than the macabre tableau that played out before them.

He wanted to scream at her but swallowed back the feeling.

"Dear Bianca," he began, the name rolling off his tongue with an artist's appreciation for beauty, "I do not expect you to understand. You never did have the perspective that I did. I have discovered our path to immortality. If my art isn't the way to be remembered, then this is." His hand swept through the air as if he were painting invisible strokes. "Once I complete this final piece, once the truth unravels and spills out into the world, they will clamor for my work."

His eyes shone with fervor, a man possessed by the certainty of his own delusion. "The value of my paintings will skyrocket. They will all want a piece of history, a fragment of the legend I will become."

A brief silence fell, punctuated only by the distant hum of the city beyond the studio walls. It was in this quiet that Ivan spotted the glint of glass on the small table by the kitchenette. He moved towards it, his footsteps measured and purposeful.

There it was, nestled between a tangle of paintbrushes and crumpled sketches—the vial of arsenic, its contents promising the permanence he craved. With a reverence reserved for the most sacred of relics, Ivan picked up the vial, feeling its weight in his hand, the cool surface belying the fiery destruction it held within.

"Ah," he exhaled softly, a twisted smile playing on his lips. "Now, we begin."

CHAPTER TWENTY SIX

Hayden parked the unmarked car at a skewed angle against the curb, its headlights cutting through the evening's gloom to illuminate the decrepit facade of the office building. Marcus, in the passenger seat, checked his weapon one last time before nodding to her. Together, they stepped into the chill that seemed to claw straight from the guts of this forsaken part of town.

"Looks abandoned," Marcus murmured, his breath fogging in the cold air as he surveyed the structure, its windows like dark, sightless eyes.

"Perfect for an artist wanting to hide away," Hayden replied, her voice a mix of dry wit and steely determination.

Deep down, she had her own doubts about this place. She had no idea what she was getting herself into, or if Ivan was even around.

They approached the sagging front doors, bypassing the remnants of a once-grand reception area. The staircase loomed before them, an ascent into uncertainty. As Hayden placed her boot on the first creaky step, the sharp scent of paint fumes hit her, the aroma unmistakable and oddly fresh amid the mustiness.

"Paint," she noted with a slight tilt of her head towards Marcus, who acknowledged with a silent grunt.

However, that didn't have to mean anything. It could be a coincidence.

Still, she felt that time was running out. She didn't know how long she had before the killer struck again.

She made her way through the door into a dimly lit hallway.

Climbing the stairs, each step felt like a move in a high-stakes chess game. Hayden let her hand drift toward her holster, comforted by the solid presence of her service pistol beneath her coat. The fumes grew stronger, guiding them like a beacon. With every floorboard that groaned underfoot, she mulled over the volatile nature of recognition, how today's masters could be tomorrow's forgotten names.

"Art and crime," Hayden mused aloud, though mostly to herself.

“Two things that don’t usually go together,” said Marcus next to her.

“Actually,” Hayden corrected, “it happens more often than you’d think. There’s a thriving black market for stolen masterpieces, usually bought by people who want a bargaining chip with the government should they ever be arrested. There’s also a huge market for forgeries.”

“Guess you’re right,” he said. “I never thought about it that way.”

“The thing about art crime is that it usually goes unnoticed. But our guy seems to want to be seen. But the problem is that both can either immortalize you or erase you,” she said.

"Deep thoughts for a moment like this," Marcus commented, a hint of humor lacing his usually stern demeanor.

She shrugged. As she moved through the hallway, careful to move quietly over the floorboards, she couldn’t help but think that this is where she belonged. As much as she loved to draw, her real calling was protecting people.

"Maybe I'm in the right line of work after all," she replied, smiling faintly at the thought. Detective work wasn't glamorous, but it was real, tangible—unlike the capricious whims of fame that seemed to govern the art world they were about to delve into.

"Let's just catch this guy," Marcus said, bringing her back to the moment, to the mission at hand.

"Agreed," Hayden said, tightening her grip on the banister as they reached the landing of the second floor. Here, the studio awaited, a breeding ground for madness or genius—or perhaps both intertwined.

They came to the door of Ivan’s studio and knocked quietly.

Hayden waited impatiently for someone to open it.

There was no answer.

She looked at Marcus and nodded. Given the urgency of the situation, there was only one course of action.

The door exploded inward under the force of Hayden's boot, splintering along the jamb with a sound that matched the pounding in her chest. Marcus's heavy steps were right on her heels as they burst into the chaos of what once was an artist's haven, now a scene of impending murder.

"Stay back!" The voice, sharp and tinged with madness, cut through the thick air. Ivan, gaunt and wild-eyed, hovered over a woman that Hayden didn’t even know he had captured.

She looked familiar, and Hayden realized that she was yet another one of his models. Her face had appeared in a painting titled “Bianca.”

Hayden assumed that was her name, since he tended to name his portraits for the people that they depicted.

Suddenly, she was glad that she had come here as soon as possible.

Bianca—the model and muse turned victim—was frozen in terror, her mouth agape in a silent scream, eyes wide and pleading.

Ivan's hand shook, dust motes of arsenic glittering in the shafts of light piercing the grimy windows. Enough poison to topple the mightiest of stallions was clutched within his grasp, and his intent was clear as he tried to steady Bianca's head with his free hand.

"Easy, easy..." Hayden's voice was calm, almost soothing, despite the adrenaline surging through her veins. Her firearm, previously aimed with lethal precision, now angled toward the ground in a gesture of peace. "Ivan, look at me."

He paused, his gaze snapping to hers, the manic energy that wrapped around him like a shroud flickering momentarily with uncertainty.

"Don't move, or I'll kill her," he said.

"Listen," she continued, taking a calculated step forward, her badge glinting dully on her belt. She lowered her gun, forcing Marcus to do the same. He gave her a confused look.

Hayden held up her hands, showing him her empty palms.

"I get it, you know? I know why you're doing this."

"How could you possibly understand?" he said. There was a tense look in his eye.

"I'm an artist too, in my own way. It is a fickle world out there, isn't it? One moment your work is hanging in the most prestigious galleries in the country; the next, you're just a name that people find vaguely familiar."

He shook with anger as she said this.

"And in a strange way, I respect what you are doing here.

The lie tasted bitter on her tongue, but Hayden knew the language of desperation, how it could twist talent into something grotesque. Marcus frowned next to her. She knew that he would want to ask what she was doing. She needed Ivan to believe her, to see her as a fellow traveler on this twisted path for recognition, not as the detective poised to end his freedom.

If she could convince him that she was on his side, then maybe she could get close enough to save Bianca before he could hurt her.

"Art is about life, about emotion," she said, her tone threaded with a feigned understanding. "And that's just what you've done. You've explored a new medium. A dark one, that lesser painters would ignore. Your work demands attention."

Ivan's grip wavered, the deadly powder seeming heavier in his hand. Hayden felt the moment teeter on a knife's edge, her words weaving a fragile truce as she held his gaze, willing him to choose art over annihilation.

Hayden's voice cut through the tense air, sharp yet oddly gentle. "But Ivan," she ventured cautiously, a ripple of strategy coursing beneath her words, "if you truly want to shock them, to make them sit up and take notice, arsenic is so passé. No one uses it in paint anymore."

Confusion flashed across Ivan's face; his attention momentarily snagged by her suggestion.

“Are you really an artist?” he said.

Hayden could almost hear the cogs turning in his twisted artist's mind, reevaluating, recalculating.

"Think about it," she pressed on, her heart thudding against her ribs like a desperate plea for time. "It's all about the spectacle, isn't it? The shock value."

Marcus, standing behind her, shifted uneasily, his eyes darting between Hayden and the man who seemed to hover between madness and clarity. Bianca's whimper punctuated the silence that followed, a soft plea for reason.

"Use a kitchen knife," Hayden said suddenly, her voice steady despite the absurdity of her own words. "It's primal, visceral. Much more... personal. It would speak volumes more than this tired method."

Ivan's head tilted, considering the detective disguised as an empathetic soul. Marcus's jaw tightened, and even Bianca, with tears streaking her face, peered at Hayden in bewildered horror. Yet there was no mistaking the potency of the ploy – the seed of doubt planted firmly in Ivan's erratic psyche.

The room held its breath, waiting on the precipice of disaster or deliverance, as Hayden's gambit teetered between brilliance and folly.

Ivan's gaze shifted from Hayden to the canvas, then back again, his brow creased in a furrow of artistic crisis. The air was thick with tension and the acrid scent of chemicals that seemed to seep into their very pores. For a moment, the deranged artist teetered on an unseen edge, swayed by the detective's audacious proposition.

"More... dramatic," he murmured, almost to himself, as he rose to his feet. The white powder clung to his fingertips, a lethal promise.

"Yes, it must be vivid... unforgettable. I always have loved the color red."

He took a step away from Bianca towards the kitchen, creating the opening that Hayden needed.

In the span of a heartbeat, Hayden seized the opening. Lunging forward, she reached for Ivan's hand, aiming to knock the arsenic away. Her fingers grazed the fine dust, and she jerked her head back, the threat of the poison's bitter kiss too close for comfort.

"Watch out!" Marcus's voice cut through the haze of danger. He sprang into action, his own body a blur of motion.

With precise timing born of years of partnership, Marcus's foot hooked around Ivan's ankle. The artist's eyes widened, a silent scream of betrayal, as his balance gave way beneath him. Time slowed as he toppled backward, the white arsenic flurrying into the air like a ghostly specter before scattering harmlessly across the stained floorboards.

The thud of Ivan's body hitting the ground was music to Hayden's ears. She pounced, her hands swift and sure as she snapped the handcuffs onto his wrists, the metallic click heralding victory. Panting, the adrenaline coursing through her veins, she stood and stepped back, eyeing her captive with a mixture of disgust and triumph.

"Gotcha," she breathed out, the weight of the chase, the fear, and the near misses lifting off her shoulders. She looked over at Marcus, who nodded, a silent communication of relief and camaraderie between them.

“What are you doing?” Ivan said, looking around wildly.

“You’re under arrest,” she said.

"Thank you," she mouthed, knowing full well Marcus’s quick thinking had made all the difference. Even though Hayden’s little plan hadn’t made sense at face value, it worked. She let Marcus call for back-up, while she went to see if Bianca was alright.

Bianca sobbed in the corner, freed from her imminent demise, but still shocked. Hayden couldn't see any initial wounds on her, and a wave of relief washed over her when she realized that she would be harmed. Hayden allowed herself a moment to feel the gravity of their success. They had caught a killer, and now they could bring solace to those haunted by his crimes. The relief was palpable, spreading warmth through her chest despite the grim surroundings.

"Let's get you booked," she said to Ivan, her voice steady now. "Your audience awaits."

EPILOGUE

The world seemed to blur and slow as Hayden stood there, the blare of sirens fading into a distant echo while she watched Bianca being carefully maneuvered into the back of an ambulance. The EMTs were methodical, their hands steady and reassuring against the backdrop of chaos that had preceded this moment. Bianca's face, pale yet composed, flickered with the kaleidoscope of red and blue lights, but her eyes met Hayden's for a fleeting second—an unspoken gratitude mingling with shock.

Hayden couldn't believe that the authorities had not even documented her kidnapping yet, and if she had been just a little bit later, things might have been much worse.

"Going to be alright," one of the paramedics assured, his voice a grounding presence as the doors clamped shut. The vehicle hummed to life, its engine a purring promise of safety and care.

Beside her, Marcus shifted his weight from one foot to another, his gaze lingering on the departing ambulance before settling on Hayden. He cleared his throat, the sound cutting through the hush that fell after the siren's cry. "You know, I wasn't sure your little plan would work. But I've got to hand it to creativity."

Hayden glanced at him, feeling the concrete cool beneath her as she leaned back against the brick wall of the building they had just exited. It still held the residual warmth from the day's sun, a stark contrast to the chill of the evening air. The night was taking over, wrapping the city in its cloak of shadows and whispered secrets.

"Sometimes you have to think outside the box," she replied, her voice steady despite the adrenaline that still coursed through her veins. "It's not about being sure; it's about taking the chance when it matters."

But the truth was, she hadn't been sure that her plan would work either. She just knew that she needed to find a way to get Ivan away from Bianca, and she followed her instincts.

Marcus nodded, the corner of his mouth twitching upward in a semblance of a smile. "Impressive, nonetheless." His hands found their way into his pockets, a familiar gesture that spoke of comfort and habit.

"Thanks," Hayden said, her attention briefly flitting back to the spot where the ambulance had been. She could still feel the residue of urgency in the air, the imprint of crisis that had called upon her to weave together threads of insight and instinct.

Around them, the city continued its nighttime symphony—cars honking, people laughing and arguing as they passed by, the distant bark of a dog. Life moved on, relentless and unabated, around two figures on the sidewalk waiting to recount the events that had unfolded behind the now silent walls of the building they guarded.

Marcus watched her with an appraising eye, the city's cacophony fading into a backdrop for this quieter moment of triumph. "You know," he began, his voice cutting through the urban din, "your methods may raise some eyebrows, Hayden, but I can't argue with results. Another case closed, thanks to your... unique approach."

Hayden fixed him with a look that held a mingling of pride and defiance. "Unorthodox, you mean?" Her hand absentmindedly traced the outline of a charcoal smudge on her jacket—a remnant of her artistic forays that often proved so instrumental in their work.

"Strange has never been a pejorative in my book," he said firmly. "Your expertise in the art world, the way you see things—it's irreplaceable. It's what cracked this one wide open."

"Thanks, Marcus." She let the words linger between them, imbued with genuine gratitude. "But remember, I'm not the only piece of the puzzle here." She glanced up at him, her eyes reflecting the neon dance of nearby signs. "For all the skepticism you throw my way, I wouldn't want anyone else by my side when we're up against the kind of darkness we face. We make quite the team."

He nodded, accepting the compliment and the responsibility it carried. In their line of work, trust was the rarest of commodities, yet here they were, two individuals whose strengths dovetailed into an effective force against those who lurked in the shadows.

"Quite the team indeed," Marcus echoed, his gaze meeting hers with renewed respect. Together, under the watchful eyes of the night, they were more than just colleagues; they were comrades in the endless battle to bring light to the darkest corners of their city.

The chill of the evening wrapped around Hayden as she watched the ambulance's taillights disappear into the distance. She drew her coat tighter, feeling the fatigue seep into her bones. The day had been a whirlwind of clues and revelations, culminating in an adrenaline-fueled confrontation. Now, with the city's symphony of sirens and car horns as a backdrop, she felt the comedown from the rush.

"Hey," Marcus said, his voice cutting through her reverie. As she turned to face him, he gestured toward a neon-lit sign across the street where a bar promised the warmth of dim lights and the clink of glasses. "How about we grab a drink? Celebrate another case closed?"

Hayden hesitated, her mind drifting to the quiet of her apartment, the familiar scent of watercolor paints, and the expectant mewling that would greet her. "I can't tonight," she replied, a small smile tugging at the corner of her lips. "I should probably get back to my apartment to feed the cat, or I might have an escape on my hands."

"Ah, duty calls." He chuckled, the sound light but understanding. "Rain check then?"

"Rain check," she confirmed, her gaze lingering on his for a moment before turning to walk away.

After finishing up the final touches of paperwork, Hayden finally made it back to her apartment. The familiar wall of suspects greeted her, as well as Pissarro the cat.

In the solitude of her apartment, Hayden dropped her keys on the counter and flicked on the lamp, bathing the space in a soft glow. Pissarro, a tabby with emerald eyes, twined around her ankles, purring his hello. After attending to his culinary demands, she sat down, the silence enveloping her like a blanket.

Her heart drummed a hesitant rhythm as she picked up her phone, thumb hovering over a contact she hadn't touched in far too long.

She was just about to get up and go to bed when her phone rang.

She looked down, expecting a call from Marcus, or even from the deputy director telling her that there was a new case already.

But to her surprise, she didn't recognize the number.

With a breath that felt like it carried the weight of a year's silence, she answered and brought the device to her ear.

"Hello?"

"Hayden!" said a voice that was vaguely familiar.

It took her a long time to place it.

But once she did, a feeling of dread washed over her.

The voice was unmistakable, warm yet threaded with surprise.

"Hi, Mom," Hayden managed, her voice steady despite the tremor of nerves. "It's been a while."

When was the last time she had spoken to her mother? It must have been at least a year.

"Hayden..." Her mother's voice softened, a mixture of emotions swirling within that single utterance of her name.

"Sorry, it's been so long," Hayden found herself saying, though the apology hung there, its context unspoken, unnecessary. There was no talk of time lost or reasons why—just the fragile bridge they were beginning to rebuild with these first, cautious words.

"How have you been?" her mother asked, genuine concern replacing the initial shock.

"Good?" she answered, not sure what to say. "Just wrapped up a case." A smile played upon her lips, invisible to her mother but no less sincere. "Things have been busy."

"Of course, darling. You always did throw yourself into your work." There was a hint of pride there, mingled with an undercurrent of something else—perhaps regret or hope, Hayden couldn't be sure.

"Are you still in LA?" Hayden asked.

"Well, that's actually why I'm calling. I've been moving around a bit more. You know me."

"Hmm." Hayden didn't know what this meant. Did her mom find a job that allowed her to travel? Did she not have a home? Hayden was too tired to ask.

"Seems that you're keeping busy," her mom said.

"Yeah, you said that already."

"I don't know how you draw criminals all day for a living. That would creep me out far too much."

"Mom, I work for the FBI now, remember? I'm not a sketch artist anymore. I went to the academy, and now I investigate cases."

"Oh, that's right. Well, listen, I'll be in the area."

Hayden bit her lip. That's what her mother had been avoiding. She took a deep breath. Perhaps it was time she made some effort to be closer to her family.

"Really? Then maybe we could meet up soon?" Hayden suggested the words leaving her lips before doubt could hold them back.

"I'd like that," her mother replied, a softness in her tone that spoke of doors left ajar, waiting to be reopened.

"Great," Hayden said, feeling a warmth spread through her chest—a cautious optimism. "I'll call again. We'll set something up."

"Take care, Hayden."

"You too, Mom." And with that, they disconnected, leaving Hayden in the quiet aftermath, pondering the steps she'd just taken towards mending bridges long thought beyond repair.

After pressing the end call button, Hayden stayed motionless, phone in hand, as the silence of the apartment enveloped her. The cat, sensing its owner's distraction, weaved figure eights around her legs, its soft fur brushing against her skin. She bent down to scoop up the feline, finding comfort in its purring presence.

Her gaze drifted to the cluttered corkboard above her desk, a mosaic of sketches and notes that had become the backdrop of her life. Amid the chaos, one area remained untouched—a small corner covered by a single photo, edges frayed, the colors faded.

It was a picture of her sister, taken the year before she vanished; her smile was the kind that reached her eyes, the sort that promised adventures and whispered secrets.

Hayden's fingers traced the outline of her sister's face as a resolve settled within her.

She knew that she wasn't supposed to work on cold cases related to family members or friends, but she knew she had to try. Maybe she could bring her family a little bit of closure. If she could untangle art forgeries and chase down thieves with little more than intuition and a keen eye, then surely, she had the skills to unearth the buried truths of her own family's mystery.

"Okay, Lila," she whispered to the photo, as if the paper could carry her words to wherever her sister might be. "Now it's your turn."

"Time to find you, sis," she said, her voice steady with purpose. She reached for her sketch pad and began to draw, not what was there, but what could be—paths not taken, leads not followed. Tonight marked the beginning of the search anew, and Hayden felt the weight of the challenge ahead.

NOW AVAILABLE!

ALL FOR NOTHING
(A Hayden Smart Mystery—Book Two)

When victims are found with stopped pocket watches, it's up to sketch artist-turned-FBI Agent Hayden Smart to draw out the truth from silent witnesses. Her sketches reveal an unsettling pattern where time stands still—but can she unlock the mystery before the killer's grand design is complete?

"A brilliant book. I couldn't put it down and I never guessed who the murderer was!"
—Reader review for Only Murder

ALL FOR NOTHING (Book 2) is the second book in a new series by #1 bestselling and critically acclaimed mystery and suspense author Rylie Dark, whose books have received over 2,000 five-star reviews and ratings. The series begins with ALL FOR ME (Book 1).

Immerse yourself in the gripping and intense world of Hayden Smart, a compelling psychological thriller series that will keep you on the edge of your seat. Follow the complex and troubled heroine through a whirlwind of relentless action, unpredictable suspense, and shocking twists. This enthralling mystery unfolds at a breathless pace, ensuring that you'll be eagerly devouring each page well into the night. Fans of Teresa Driscoll, Melinda Leigh, and Kendra Elliot are sure to fall in love.

Future books in the series are also available.

"I loved this thriller, read it in one sitting. Lots of twists and turns and I didn't guess the
culprit at all… Already pre-ordered the second!"
—Reader review for Only Murder

"This book takes off with a bang… An excellent read, and I'm looking forward to the next book!"
—Reader review for SEE HER RUN

“Fantastic book! It was hard to put down. I can’t wait to see what happens next!”
—Reader review for SEE HER RUN

“The twists and turns kept coming. Can't wait to read the next book!”
—Reader review for SEE HER RUN

“A must-read if you enjoy action-packed stories with good plots!”
—Reader review for SEE HER RUN

“I really like this author and this series starts with a bang. It will keep you turning the pages till the end of the book and wanting more.”
—Reader review for SEE HER RUN

“I can't say enough about this author! How about ‘out of this world’! This author is going to go far!”
—Reader review for ONLY MURDER

“I really enjoyed this book… The characters were alive, and the twists and turns were great. It will keep you reading till the end and leave you wanting more.”
—Reader review for NO WAY OUT

“This is an author that I highly recommend. Her books will have you begging for more.”
—Reader review for NO WAY OUT

Rylie Dark

Bestselling author Rylie Dark is author of the SADIE PRICE FBI SUSPENSE THRILLER series, comprising six books; of the CARLY SEE FBI SUSPENSE THRILLER series, comprising six books; of the MIA NORTH FBI SUSPENSE THRILLER series, comprising six books; of the MORGAN STARK FBI SUSPENSE THRILLER series, comprising five books; of the HAILEY ROCK FBI SUSPENSE THRILLER series, comprising eight books; of the TARA STRONG MYSTERY series, comprising six books; of the ALEX QUINN FBI SUSPENSE THRILLER series, comprising five books; of the MAEVE SHARP FBI SUSPENSE THRILLER, comprising five books; of the KELLY CRUZ FBI SUSPENSE THRILLER, comprising five books; of the JESSIE REACH FBI SUSPENSE THRILLER, comprising seven books (and counting); of the BECCA THORN FBI SUSPENSE THRILLER, comprising five books (and counting); of the CASEY FAITH SUSPENSE THRILLER, comprising five books (and counting); of the ARIA BRANDT SUSPENSE THRILLER, comprising five books (and counting); and of the new HAYDEN SMART SUSPENSE THRILLER, comprising five books (and counting).

An avid reader and lifelong fan of the mystery and thriller genres, Rylie loves to hear from you, so please feel free to visit www.ryliedark.com to learn more and stay in touch.

BOOKS BY RYLIE DARK

HAYDEN SMART MYSTERY
ALL FOR ME (Book #1)
ALL FOR NOTHING (Book #2)
ALL FOR VENGEANCE (Book #3)
ALL FOR YOU (Book #4)
ALL FOREVER (Book #5)

ARIA BRANDT MYSTERY
THE UNKNOWN WOMAN (Book #1)
THE UNKNOWN WIFE (Book #2)
THE UNKNOWN NEIGHBOR (Book #3)
THE UNKNOWN GUEST (Book #4)
THE UNKNOWN PAST (Book #5)

CASEY FAITH MYSTERY
BEHIND HIS EYES (Book #1)
BEHIND HIS SMILE (Book #2)
BEHIND HIS MASK (Book #3)
BEHIND HIS LIES (Book #4)
BEHIND HIS THOUGHTS (Book #5)

BECCA THORN MYSTERY
GONE COLD (Book #1)
GONE DARK (Book #2)
GONE SILENT (Book #3)
GONE HOLLOW (Book #4)
GONE FOREVER (Book #5)

JESSIE REACH MYSTERY
HIS OTHER SIDE (Book #1)
HIS OTHER SELF (Book #2)
HIS OTHER SECRET (Book #3)
HIS OTHER WISH (Book #4)
HIS OTHER PLAN (Book #5)

KELLY CRUZ MYSTERY
WHERE YOU GO (Book #1)
WHERE YOU HIDE (Book #2)
WHERE YOU SLEEP (Book #3)
WHERE YOU RUN (Book #4)
WHERE YOU FEAR (Book #5)

MAEVE SHARP FBI SUSPENSE THRILLER
WITH MALICE (Book #1)
WITH ENVY (Book #2)
WITH VENGEANCE (Book #3)
WITH RAGE (Book #4)
WITH YOU (Book #5)

ALEX QUINN SUSPENSE THRILLER
FIRST, MURDER (Book #1)
SECOND, DEATH (Book #2)
THIRD, ENVY (Book #3)
FOURTH, LUST (Book #4)
FIFTH, WRATH (Book #5)

TARA STRONG MYSTERY
GIRL WITHOUT A CHANCE (Book #1)
GIRL WITHOUT A HOME (Book #2)
GIRL WITHOUT A TRACE (Book #3)
GIRL WITHOUT A NAME (Book #4)
GIRL WITHOUT A PRAYER (Book #5)
GIRL WITHOUT A PAST (Book #6)

HAILEY ROCK FBI SUSPENSE THRILLER
BEHIND YOU (Book #1)
BESIDE YOU (Book #2)
AFTER YOU (Book #3)
WATCHING YOU (Book #4)
JUDGING YOU (Book #5)
FOLLOWING YOU (Book #6)

SADIE PRICE FBI SUSPENSE THRILLER
ONLY MURDER (Book #1)
ONLY RAGE (Book #2)

ONLY HIS (Book #3)
ONLY ONCE (Book #4)
ONLY SPITE (Book #5)
ONLY MADNESS (Book #6)

MIA NORTH FBI SUSPENSE THRILLER
SEE HER RUN (Book #1)
SEE HER HIDE (Book #2)
SEE HER SCREAM (Book #3)
SEE HER VANISH (Book #4)
SEE HER GONE (Book #5)
SEE HER DEAD (Book #6)

CARLY SEE FBI SUSPENSE THRILLER
NO WAY OUT (Book #1)
NO WAY BACK (Book #2)
NO WAY HOME (Book #3)
NO WAY LEFT (Book #4)
NO WAY UP (Book #5)
NO WAY TO DIE (Book #6)

MORGAN STARK FBI SUSPENSE THRILLER
TOO LATE (Book #1)
TOO CLOSE (Book #2)
TOO FAR GONE (Book #3)
TOO LOST (Book #4)
TOO BROKEN (Book #5)

Printed in Great Britain
by Amazon

58702191R00091